LADY FIRST

"What are you doi[ng...] Vanderkloot, after s[he stri]pped him naked.

"Um, nothing," the anthropologist said.

"You're holding a pencil against my tool," Remo pointed out. "I don't exactly call that nothing."

Naomi withdrew the pencil and used it to scribble a single digit number onto the notepad by her pillow.

"Want to take my temperature, too?" muttered Remo.

"I already know your temperature," Naomi said. "You're *hot*. Like me."

Her look made it clear that Naomi demanded one thing more before she told Remo what he desperately needed to know. Remo had to make love before he could make war. . . .

Destroyer

#80

DEATH SENTENCE

Created by

WARREN MURPHY & RICHARD SAPIR

A SIGNET BOOK

Published by the Penguin Group
Penguin Books USA Inc., 375 Hudson Street,
New York, New York 10014, U.S.A.
Penguin Books Ltd, 27 Wrights Lane,
London W8 5TZ, England
Penguin Books Australia Ltd, Ringwood,
Victoria, Australia
Penguin Books Canada Ltd, 2801 John Street,
Markham, Ontario, Canada L3R 1B4
Penguin Books (N.Z.) Ltd, 182-190 Wairau Road,
Auckland 10, New Zealand

Penguin Books Ltd, Registered Offices:
Harmondsworth, Middlesex, England

First Printing, April, 1990
10 9 8 7 6 5 4 3 2 1

 REGISTERED TRADEMARK—MARCA REGISTRADA

Printed in the United States of America

For Lee Weeks, who set the lions at the Folcroft gates.

And for the amazing Jim O'Connor, who rescued this novel from electronic oblivion.

And for the Glorious House of Sinanju, P.O. Box 2505, Quincy, MA 02269.

1

Naomi Vanderkloot knew people.

Hers was not an instinctual knowledge. She possessed no innate ability to read faces, voices, or personalities. In truth, she couldn't tell if a fellow human being were telling the truth three times out of ten, if her personal life was any barometer.

Naomi Vanderkloot knew people. She just didn't understand them. This was because everything Naomi Vanderkloot knew about people came from books.

As she turned in her chair to look out the bunkerlike window of her office, she wondered, for the first time in her thirty-three years on earth, if perhaps that was the problem.

Her thin eyebrows slowly drew together as she stared past the stark black-and-white geometry of the Kennedy Library to Boston harbor, believed by some voters to be radioactive. Today the harbor was slate gray. The sky above was the same uncertain near-blue of Naomi Vanderkloot's sad eyes.

They were the eyes that beheld the secret initiation rites of the Moomba tribe of the Philippines. They were the eyes of the first white person to behold, however briefly in the lightning-illuminated Matto Grosso, a member of the semilegendary Xitlis.

They were also the eyes that had sized up Randy Gunsmith, all six-foot-five and 228 pounds of gorgeous unemployed construction worker, as well as the petite blond on his arm, and not questioned the lack of family resemblance when Randy fumblingly introduced the blond as his sister Candy from Evansville, Indiana.

The occasion had been the previous Friday night. Naomi had left her office in the anthropology department of the University of Massachusetts and taken the Red Line subway to Harvard Square. She had been walking down Church Street when Randy and his "sister" unexpectedly emerged from Passim's, a popular coffee shop.

At first Randy had appeared flustered. Naomi had been so self-absorbed—her normal state of mind—that it wasn't until three days later, when she returned to her Brattle Street apartment early and found Randy spooning Cool Whip onto the hollow between his "sister's" lush breasts, that she recalled his surprised expression.

"Oh, my God," Naomi said. "You're doing it with your sister."

"Don't be a complete idiot, Naomi," Randy had snapped back as he covered himself with a sheet. "She's no more my sister than you are."

"Oh," Naomi said, getting it at last.

It wasn't the fact that her boyfriend had been cheating on her that bothered Naomi Vanderkloot as much as it was that he covered himself up. As if he were ashamed or unwilling for her to behold him in what Naomi used to playfully call his "tumescent state."

She realized then—one of the few flashes of insight she would show in her life—that she had seen his magnificent male tool for the last time. And that realization brought her to her knees at the side of the bed. Her bed.

"Please, Randy don't leave me!" she wailed.

"Great, now you want me," he muttered. "If you'd paid half as much attention to me as your stupid hypotheses, I wouldn't have had to go looking for a little satisfaction in the first place."

"I know! I know!" Naomi had cried, her voice as abject as a temple votary. More abject. Naomi had met temple votaries. They were much more dignified than she was. She clenched at the blanket in an effort to keep him from leaving.

But Randy Gunsmith had no intention of leaving. He hadn't finished yet.

"Mind waiting outside, Naomi?" he said.

"But . . . but this is my apartment!" she had sputtered.

"Ten minutes. That's all. Then we can discuss this. I promise. Okay?"

Her lower lip quivering, Naomi Vanderkloot nodded mutely. She couldn't muster the nerve to speak. She was afraid her voice would crack.

Stiffly she closed the bedroom door behind her and slumped in a director's chair. She fingered the spines of the many volumes that crowded the concrete-block bookcases in her living room, her fingers lingering over *The Naked Ape* and other books that had inspired her life and career.

When Randy Gunsmith finally emerged, not ten or even fifteen minutes later, but after a full sigh-and-groan-punctuated hour, he was fully dressed and pulled the blond along after him.

Naomi Vanderkloot shot to her feet, her nails digging into the palms of her bony hands. Her mouth parted. But before she could form a single uncertain syllable, Randy shot her a curt "Later" and slammed the front door behind him.

Through the beaded curtains Naomi watched them hurry, hand in hand, past the Victorian homes of her upscale Cambridge neighborhood.

She knew then that she would never see him again.

At first Naomi blamed her preoccupation with her

latest researches for the breakup. Hurt, she couldn't look at her papers and clippings for nearly twelve hours.

Then in the middle of the night she threw back the covers that she hadn't bothered to change because they still had Randy's Coors-and-Winston scent on them and plunged back into her work. If her work had caused another romance to fail, then she was determined to make that work the most important of her life.

It was looking now, on the Monday following those unsettling events, as if the months of work she had put into her latest theory was about to slide into the loss column too.

The knock on her office door brought Naomi out of her reverie. She swiveled in her chair. Her hurt expression melted and rehardened into a cool professional mask. She adjusted her owl-round glasses on her straight nose, and automatically her parted mouth sealed primly. She patted at her mouse-brown hair and called, "Yes, come in."

Even before the door yawned open, she knew what kind of an expression the reporter would be wearing. She had seen it a thousand times before. No innate knowledge of the male animal was required. Only endless repetitive experience.

The man was tall and slim. Not terribly distinguished, but Naomi, recalling his journalistic affiliation, suddenly realized that she was lucky to pull a primate above the knuckle-walking stage.

He poked his head around the doorjamb expectedly, his face curious, even hopeful.

The moment his eyes focused on her, the expression dropped away, leaving a vaguely disappointed one.

It was a transmutation Naomi Vanderkloot knew well. It marked, to the microsecond, the precise moment the male brain realized that it was seeing, not a nubile Naomi, but a knobby Vanderkloot.

Naomi let out a tiny sigh that collapsed her sunken bosom more severely than normal.

"Hello," she said in her prim, not-quite-cold, but distinctly unwarm voice. She rose awkwardly, all six-foot-two of her. "You must be Mearle." She offered a cool hand in a gesture midway between a handshake and the expectation of a hand kiss.

The man shook it. He did not kiss it.

"That's me," Mearle told her as she smoothed the back of her severe black skirt and resumed her seat. Mearle dropped into a plain chair. He looked about the office, evidently finding it more interesting than its occupant. Or possibly just less hard on the eyes.

"I can't believe I'm actually going through with this," Naomi said to break the silence.

Mearle's eyes refocused. He was an ectomorph. Naomi noticed his long tapering fingers, often found on writers and artists. Probably a fast sugar burner, she thought.

"This what?" Mearle asked a little vaguely, and Naomi reconsidered her assessement.

"This interview," she reminded him coolly. "It's the reason you've came, isn't it?"

"Actually, I'm here because my editor told me to come."

Naomi's voice dropped ten degrees. "Well, I'll try not to take up too much of your precious time."

"What?" He was staring at a chart illustrating the evolution of the human animal from *Homo habilis* to modern *Homo sapiens*. He pointed to the full-frontal-nude drawing labeled "*Homo Erectus*," and remarked, "No wonder the queers leave the broads alone. When they get it up, it's nothing."

" '*Homo Erectus*' is Latin for 'Man the Erect,' " Naomi told him reprovingly. "He was the first of our primate ancestors to walk upright. I can't believe people don't know these fundamental things. This is your species."

"Are you calling me a homo, lady? Because if you are, I'll be glad to demonstrate that I can get it up."

"No, no, don't," Naomi said, shielding her eyes. "Can we simply get on with this?"

"Hold on a minute, will you?" Mearle fumbled through his coat pockets, seemingly having trouble getting those intelligent-looking fingers past his lapels.

Definitely a slow sugar burner, Naomi decided. It was unusual. Statistically, most slow sugar burners had stubby, blunt fingers. She made a mental note of the discrepancy, and decided to pay closer attention to the man's mannerisms. Perhaps an unusual phenotypical pattern might emerge.

Finally Mearle located his mini cassette tape recorder and placed in on the corner of Naomi's desk. Its spools turned silently.

"I rather imagined you'd use a pad and paper."

"Don't know shorthand," Mearle told her.

"Were you considered slow as a child, Mr. . . . ?"

Mearle didn't pick up on the lead. Instead he said, "I don't remember. My editor says you've made an important discovery."

"Yes, I have. But before I start, it's important that you know my background. So you know I'm not some wild-eyed theoretician. I'm a professor of anthropology. Harvard, class of seventy-nine. I've done extensive fieldwork in Asia, Africa, and South America."

"How do you spell that?"

"Spell what?"

"Anthology."

"Anthropology. It's from the Greek. It means the study of man. I study men."

Mearle's eyebrows shot up. "No women?"

"I study women too. By man, we anthropologists refer to man the species. It's not supposed to be a gender-specific term."

"Think you can use smaller words, Professor

Vanderkloot? Our readers are not exactly swift in the brain department."

"Slow sugar burners, you mean?" This time it was Naomi's brows that lifted.

"Say again?"

"It's been discovered that the human brain processes glucose—natural sugar—at greatly different speeds. Some people process their brain sugar very rapidly. Consequently, these people are very quick thinkers. Others, whose brains are less efficient, seem to be slower-witted."

Mearle the reporter perked up, interest lighting his dull face.

"Great! That's exactly the kind of angle our readers love."

"Really?"

"Yeah. I can see a great headline: ANTHOLOGY PROFESSOR MAKES STARTLING ANNOUNCEMENT: ALL-SUGAR DIET INCREASES BRAINPOWER."

Naomi's brows fell sharply. "That's *not* what I meant," she said.

"I eat a lot of sugar," Mearle went on as if he hadn't heard. "I guess that explains why I'm so smart."

"Do your friends and family consider you very intelligent?"

"Sure. I'm a writer. I make a lot of money."

"Journalist, you mean."

"Lady," Mearle said sternly, "I've been with the *National Enquirer* since eighty-three, and in all that time I never once saw a journalist darken my editor's door. Any unimaginative fool can copy down quotes and string them into a newspaper article. We're writers. We make the dull facts jump up and grab you by the throat. That's what sells newspapers."

"And used cars," Naomi said dryly.

"I used to write confession stories before this," Mearle said, not understanding. "It's the same technique. This is easier. I don't have to make everything up from scratch. So okay, let's get back to this sugar thing. What would it do to the average person's IQ if he doubled his sugar intake? If you don't know, try to guess on the high side, okay?"

"Oh, the average American would probably burn out the adrenal glands," Naomi said airily.

"Is that good or bad?"

"In your case, it would probably be an improvement," she said sarcastically. She regretted the lapse almost as soon as she uttered it. Fortunately Mearle No-last-name, Boston stringer for the *National Enquirer*, took it as a compliment.

"Really?" he said with ill-disguised interest. He was fascinated. "Maybe I'll triple my sugar intake."

"Let me know how it turns out." And this time Naomi smiled. Her lips resembled a rubber band stretching, right to the dull red color. No hint of teeth showed.

"I love sugar. Always have."

Naomi went on doggedly, "It's important that the world understand my credentials. I was the first white person to see a member of the Xitli tribe. I, and I alone, have been initiated into the Moomba secret ceremony."

"Great! We'll do a sidebar. Let's hear all the gory details."

"I'd rather not get into that," Naomi said quickly, a flicker of embarrassment flooding her ordinarily bloodless features. "What I'm trying to tell you is that before I returned to academe . . . er, teaching full-time, I was a highly respected field anthropologist. *Not* a crackpot."

"Can I quote that last statement?"

Naomi made a prim face. "Please don't." She cleared her throat and went on. "For the last five years I've taught courses in political anthropology, imperialism and ethnocentrism, and ecological anthropology. I also consult for IHPA, the Institute for Human Potential Awareness. It was while compiling data for that organization that I first discovered that *he* exists."

Mearle, catching the portentous tone of the pronoun, jumped to the slow-sugar conclusion.

"He? Do you mean God?"

"I definitely do *not* mean God. I'm an atheist."

"Can you spell that?"

"Look it up. You'll find a definition that goes with it."

"Good thinking." Mearle grabbed the tape recorder and spoke loudly into it, "Look up 'atheist' for spelling and definition. Okay, go ahead," he told Naomi, replacing the machine.

Naomi plowed ahead. "It began when I took on the task of sorting newspaper clippings and other accounts of extraordinary human physical achievement."

"I can wriggle my ears," Mearle piped up. "One of them, anyway. The left. No, it's the right."

Seeing Naomi's expression, he subsided, one ear quivering.

"In these instances we were dealing with incidents of heightened strength or reflexes," Naomi went on in her best lecturer's voice. "Perhaps you've heard stories of ordinary people who become empowered with near-superhuman strength in times of stress. Like the mother who discovers her child trapped under a car. In her anxiousness, she upends the vehicle to rescue the child."

"I once did a story along those lines. ENRAGED GRANDMOTHER LOSES CAN OPENER, BITES BOTTLE TOP OFF WITH FALSE TEETH. Like that?"

"Not quite. And could you please stop interrupting? This is very important to me."

"If it were that important, you'd be talking to *Scientific American*, not me."

Naomi made a face. "They declined to publish my findings," she admitted in a morose tone. "So I went down the list of national magazines, then local newspapers. The Boston *Globe* actually sent out a reporter, but after twenty minutes he pretended he was late to an interview with a local television anchor. I went to the *Herald* next, and even they weren't interested. I thought I had hit bottom; then I remembered you people."

"Actually, we lead our field. You should see our competition. Some of them don't bother getting quotes. They make 'em up."

"I want my story to get out, Mr. . . ."

"Call me Mearle. 'Mister' makes me think I'm being lectured."

"As I was saying, I want my story to get out. It's important. For if my data are correct, mankind may be on the threshold of an important new era in its evolution." Her tone darkened. "Or, conversely, we may face the extinction of the human race."

"Oh, my God," Mearle said in genuine horror. "Are we facing a global sugar shortage? Will our brains shrivel?"

"Forget sugar!" Naomi snapped. "We're talking about superman."

"We are?"

"We are. You surely know something about evolution. How we as a species have evolved from a manlike ape ancestor."

"Darwin."

"Yes, Darwin. Mankind has come a long way on the evolutionary scale, but it's not over yet. Have you ever wondered about the next step?"

"No."

"No. No one wonders. It took millions of years for man to learn to walk erect, to develop the cranial capacity to house a manlike brain, to generate prehensile fingers and an opposable thumb. No one is quite certain how these developments occurred. They are still the subject of raging debate because they are

not sudden occurrences. They happen over generations. Well, Mearle, I have discovered that the next
stage in human evolution has already arrived. Now.
Here in the U.S."

"I'll bet it's all that sugar we eat. It probably accel-
erates the process."

"Could I tell this? . . . Thank you. At the Institute
for Human Potential Awareness I went through literally tens of thousands of accounts of extraordinary
human feats. I sorted them according to sex. Then
within gender. I divided those accounts into incidents of accelerated reflex, heightened strength, and
other like phenomena. Many of these incidents are
easily explained with the parameters of known physi-
ology. Adrenaline can convey great strength for short
periods of time. High-speed mental calculations are
possible by some brains—oddly, most of these are
people who suffer from forms of retardation. Other
traits are the product of a dominant gene that can
disappear for generations."

"You're losing me."

"I'm just getting to my point," Naomi said quickly.
"As I sorted these accounts, I was struck by certain
commonalities among them. Do you remember the
Yuma Emergency last Christmas?"

"Who doesn't? An American city taken over by a
Japanese movie company. It was worse than the
Chinese student massacres."

"The government hushed a lot of it up. But several
eyewitness accounts made it into Arizona newspapers,
and these came into my hands. During the height of
the crisis, many people reported that the occupying
army was attacked and virtually dismantled."

"By U.S. Rangers," Mearle said flatly.

"That's Washington's cover story," Naomi countered.
"I personally flew to Yuma to interview some of the
eyewitnesses, and they described to me a lone man
who tore tanks apart, bested squads of heavily armed

Japanese troops, and virtually lifted the siege of Yuma
with his bare hands. *Before* the Rangers parachuted
in."

"One man?" Mearle said skeptically.

"One *unarmed* man. A man who, by all accounts,
was six feet tall and weighed no more than one
hundred and sixty pounds. What we anthropologists
call an ectomorph."

"I'll look it up."

"No need. An ectomorph is a thin person. An
endomorph is a fat person. And a mesomorph is a
normally muscled person."

"Which am I?"

"A biped. Barely."

"I'll look it up."

"Do." Naomi smiled fiercely. "This man was a
casuasoid. Slim. Obviously not the weight-lifter type.
Yet he bent gun barrels in his fingers. Bullets could
not stop him."

"They're supposed to bounce off Superman."

"I have no reports of such a phenomenon. He
evidently avoided them by pure reflex."

"Adrenaline or sugar?"

"Neither. This man sustained these impossible activities. Adrenaline is good for twenty-minute stretches.
This man—this seemingly ordinary man—systemati-
cally dismantled the Japanese army in the course of a
long day of hand-to-hand fighting. The reports described him as unremarkable except for two distin-
guishing features that stuck in the minds of the people
who witnessed his destructive power. He had unusually thick wrists. And his eyes were dead."

Mearle gulped in spite of himself. "Dead?"

"Flat. Lifeless. Devoid of emotion. That kind of
dead."

"I don't get it."

"There's more. Before I flew to Yuma to check out
these reports firsthand, I collected all the Yuma re-

ports and checked for similar reports elsewhere. I found them. Clipped from obscure newspapers and journals. Some of the sources were pretty disreputable. *Fate* magazine. The *Fortean Journal.* Publications that revel in ghosts and UFO's and Bigfeet."

"Foot. Bigfoot. Actually, I did a poll on UFO's. Do you know that over seventy-seven percent of Americans believe in flying saucers?"

"You people actually conducted a nationwide survey?"

"No," Mearle said casually. "We sampled an Akron neighborhood and extrapolated from there."

"That's statistically unsupportable!"

Mearle shrugged. "It sold papers."

"I'm sure that it did," Naomi said acidly. "In any case, I found other reports of incredible feats. All of them had one thing in common. The man who performed them had thick wrists and dark dead eyes. Sometimes he was not alone, but was accompanied by an enigmatic Asian. I don't understand that part myself. I doubt they could be related or even part of the same gene pool. Yet both performed similar extraordinary feats. And these reports come from all over America."

"This is great. This is wonderful," enthused Mearle, for the first time checking his tape recorder to see if it was running. It was.

"You see what I am leading up to?"

"Yeah! Space aliens. They're probably after our sugar."

"I am *not* talking about aliens," Naomi snorted. "I was trying to communicate to you that the next stage in human evolution has appeared in our society. In America. Now. The man who will lead humanity into the twenty-first century. The man who, once he begins to sow his seed, will usher in a new race of men, making all of us poor ethnocentric *Homo sapiens* as obsolete as *Australopithecus.*"

"He's a farmer?"

"I had another kind of seed in mind. Sperm."

"Now I get it. He's a menace. Are you saying he should be destroyed before he breeds?"

"No. never. If this man is the next step in evolution, it will be up to us, as the former dominant species, to step aside, just as the Neanderthal man stepped aside for Cro-Magnon."

"That's crazy!"

"To the contrary. Evolution is wonderfully sane. And so am I. In fact, I would volunteer in a moment to bear the child of this next stage of *Homo sapiens*. It would be a privilege."

Mearle blinked. "That's what you want me to write? That you're looking for a date?"

Naomi's shark-fin face grew sharper. "That was very crudely put," she said primly. "This is science. This is the future."

"No," returned Mearle, shutting off his tape recorder as he got to his feet. "This is the front page of our next issue."

"Wait! Don't you want to hear the rest of my hypothesis?"

"Later. My editor is sure to want follow-up. Right now, I've got more than I need."

The door slammed after him, stirring the mousy tendrils of hair that framed Naomi Vanderkloot's narrow forehead like venetian-blind cords.

"I hope I haven't made a big mistake," she muttered under her breath. "I'm up for tenure next year. . . ."

Buddy Newman was expecting the gray man.

On the third Tuesday of every month, the Sak-N-Sav where Buddy was a cashier ran a two-for-one special on certain slow-moving products, among them Flako Magic Potato Mix. It was the Flako that brought the gray man into the store, where once a month he invariably stocked up, buying as many as six boxes at a time.

After three years of ringing up the gray man's third-Tuesday purchases—all on sale and most unfit for discriminating stomachs—Buddy Newman looked forward to seeing the gray man the way he looked forward to registering for the draft. Not as bad as a root canal, but it was no walk in the park either.

So when the gray man came in through the photoelectric doors and made a beeline for the sale aisle, Buddy Newman groaned inwardly.

Buddy thought of him as the gray man even though he knew his name was Smith. Buddy knew that fact because he lived on the same street as the man, in Rye, New York. The front-door nameplate of the Tudor-style house said: Smith. That was as much about him as Buddy Newman knew or wanted to know.

Smith was not exactly the kind of person you'd invite over for a barbecue. He was a dry, lanky cut of a man who always wore a gray three-piece suit and the same striped school tie. His hair was the dirty white of a thin stormcloud. His eyes were gray. Even his skin was gray. That was the truly unappetizing thing about the man, that lizardy gray skin.

As the gray man named Smith emerged from the aisle, hugging exactly eight boxes of Flako Magic Potato Mix under his bony Adam's apple, Buddy Newman gave out a little groan.

There were six cashiers at the Sak-N-Save, and Buddy had the express aisle. Eight items or less. He sighed.

The gray man set the boxes down on the conveyor belt and reached into his pocket, extracting a worn leather wallet. Buddy began running the boxes past the optical bar-code reader, knowing that even before his register totaled up the amount, the gray man would have arrived at the correct figure mentally. Buddy knew this because the man invariably counted out the exact change before Buddy had a machine total. Once the man had insisted that Buddy's cash register was in error. Buddy politely told him that the bar-code reader did not make mistakes.

The gray man had insisted in a lemony voice and Buddy had had to call the manager. It was Buddy's first month on the job and he hadn't yet learned how to deal with troublesome customers. He hoped that the manager would toss the gray man out into the parking lot.

Instead, the gray man pointed to a flawed bar code on one box and impatiently stood by while the manager entered the cost by hand. He then reprimanded Buddy for not having the sense to simply hit the repeat key after the scanner picked the price off the first box.

Buddy actually turned beet-red at that, his first reprimand. He never again forgot to use the repeat key.

But this time Buddy deliberately didn't hit the repeat key. Let the guy suffer, he thought, just as he himself suffered every time the gray man pulled out his red change holder and counted out exact change with maddening care. That was the thing that drove Buddy crazy. Anyone else would be content to slap down two or three quarters and accept the change. The man insisted on counting out every last penny, no matter how much he had to scrounge in that ridiculous plastic change holder.

So this time Buddy took his time totaling the bill. Maybe the gray man—whose skin looked even grayer than usual today—would take his purchases to another register next time.

The man clutched his change in hand while Buddy pretended to have trouble with the scanner. He knew from long practice how to hold the box so that it would misread. He did this repeatedly.

"Hold the box flatter," the gray man suggested in a voice that sounded as if it had been squeezed from a lemon peel.

"Sorry, sir," Buddy said, secretly glad that he had touched a nerve. He fussed with the box, noting the thinning of the man's bloodless lips. He noticed again the flat grayness of his skin. Normally it was the color of fish skin. Tonight it resembled pencil lead.

As the gray man squirmed impatiently, his eyes wandered to the magazine rack, where the latest editions of the women's magazines and various tabloids screamed their coverlines.

The gray man did a comical double-take. One gray hand reached out for the latest *Enquirer* with shocking urgency. He took in the cover with eyes that showed white all the way around behind the transparent shields of his rimless glasses. He tore the paper open, searching for something. When he found what he sought, his skin went even grayer, if anything, and his eyes wider.

Buddy Newman was so surprised at this uncharacteristic behavior that he actually stopped working and looked at the man in wonderment. It was the shortest-lived expression that Buddy Newman ever had on his face.

For the gray man suddenly clutched at his chest, the pages of the *Enquirer* scattering like origami pigeons. His mouth went wide. His lips and fingernails seemed almost blue. His eyes strained from their sockets like hard-boiled eggs from a clenched fist, and the gray man folded like a lawn chair, landing on the conveyor belt. He was carried along until he jammed up against the coupon shelf in a welter of limbs.

Buddy Newman recognized the signs of a heart attack from his CPR class and hit the manager's bell. Without waiting, he flipped the gray man around so

that he could get to his face. It was as gray as a
corpse's face now.

Buddy pinched off the nose and pried open the
man's gasping mouth, checking first to see that he
hadn't swallowed his tongue. He hadn't. It lay in his
mouth, a fat gray slug. Steeling himself for the dis-
tastefulness of his task, Buddy pressed his mouth to
the gray man's lips. They were turning a grayish-
blue. He exhaled forcefully, withdrew, then repeated
the procedure.

The manager hurried up and Buddy shouted to
him, "Call an ambulance! He's dying!" Then he put
his lips to those of the gray man named Smith.
Smith's lips were cold as fresh cod. And just about as
tasty. Buddy forced more air into the unresponsive
lungs, hot tears in his eyes.

After the ambulance attendants had wheeled the
gray man out the electric doors, Buddy sat on the
conveyor belt that normally carried apples and dough-
nuts and pork chops to their ultimate destiny and
listened silently to the manager's distant but reassuring voice telling him that he would probably receive
some kind of commendation from the chain, if the
customer survived.

Buddy didn't think the man would survive. The
cold taste on his lips made him feel as if he'd kissed a
corpse.

Finally, after Buddy had calmed down, the manager sent him home early. Buddy took with him a
copy of the *Enquirer*.

There were several headlines, Buddy saw as he
walked to his house. One of them, he felt, had
caused the man to have a heart attack.

Buddy instantly dismissed the top headline, which
informed the world, STARTLING NEW EVIDENCE! SAME
ASSASSIN KILLED ROY ORBISON, LUCILLE BALL, AND
AYATOLLAH KHOMEINI!"

There was a box item that promised to reveal the

secret of the *Enquirer* All-Pizza Weight-Loss Program. Smith hadn't looked as if he'd ever eaten a pizza in his life.

That left only one other story. The headline read: AMAZING TRUTH REVEALED. EVOLUTIONARY SUPERMAN LOOSE IN U.S.!

Below that was an artist's rendition of a man's cruel face. He had high cheekbones and the deadest eyes Buddy had ever seen. Even in the sketch, those eyes seemed to bore through Buddy's shaken soul like drill bits.

He opened to the inside page and by the lights of passing streetlamps read about the being whom the reporter had dubbed "Dead Man," who, if the reports could be believed, roamed the streets of America committing actions of indescribable violence. It sounded to Buddy like someone's idea for a bad comic book. Then he looked back at the dead eyes that stared out from the cover and shuddered uncontrollably.

No wonder Smith had keeled over. The guy looked like death personified.

Convinced he had solved the mystery of Smith's apparent heart attack, Buddy Newman hurried to his parents' house and had nightmares in which the express-line conveyor belt was choked with corpses who clutched alien coins while Buddy frantically tried to bag them before they died on him.

2

His name was Remo and the sound of the buzzer snapped him from sleep.

He lay there, letting his slow-to-focus brown eyes take in the unfamiliar surroundings. He didn't recognize the ceiling. It was too white. He blinked, and sat up slowly. His head hurt. There was a dull pain in back of his deep-set eyes. It felt like the optic nerves had been seared and not quite healed.

He rolled to the side of the lumpy cot and took his head in his hands. When he lifted his face, he looked around the cell, which was illuminated by the strong light from outside the bars.

It was a bare cell. The walls were pink-painted cinder block and in one corner was a stainless-steel toilet with a broken sink atop the water tank. Other than the cot and the toilet, the cell was as barren as a bald man's scalp. And just as pink.

Remo stood up in his boxer shorts and relieved himself into the lidless toilet. He stared at the wall as if trying to comprehend it. After he buttoned up, he found his blue work uniform folded on the floor, his leather state-issue shoes resting on the neat pile. He put on the pants first and then laced his shoes. They were new and felt like diver's weighted shoes when he took a tentative step around the six-by-nine cell.

Down the corridor he heard the sound of men, like himself, stirring in their confined spaces. A black voice cursed the new day bitterly. A younger voice

26

simply broke down and sobbed. Jeers replied with a callousness that beggared understanding.

And mixed in with those rude sounds were those of footsteps. Booted feet. Free feet. Feet walking the corridor unfettered and heading in his direction.

"Head count!" an authoritarian voice barked. "Sound off!"

"Fuck you, man!" another voice challenged. The booted feet stopped. There was a pause. Then the same voice answered again, this time more submissively: "Number Eighty."

Other voices called out: "Number Fifty-five." "Number Thirty-seven." "Number one-eighty-one."

Finally, as Remo buttoned his short-sleeved workshirt, the feet stopped at the bars of his cell.

There were two sets of them. The two men wore identical gray uniform shirts with black epaulets and pocket trim. Their pants were black, with charcoal-gray stripes running down the outer seams. Their Smokey the Bear hats were black and shaded hard mean eyes.

"How was your first night, Dead Man?" the taller of the two correction officers asked without looking up from his clipboard.

"Bend over and I'll show you," Remo snarled. Their accents were all wrong. Too southern. And the uniform colors were not right either. The thought sank into his mind slowly, like a water lily losing its buoyancy.

"Yeah," the second C.O. said. He was nearly as wide as he was tall, and he was not tall. "I heard you were a tough SOB."

"The name is Remo."

"You mean Convict Number Six."

"That's not my number."

"Up in New Jersey, maybe. But down here, you're Number Six. Now, stand back from those bars, boy. The warden wants to see you."

Remo let go of the bars and stepped back as the
C.O. called down to the watch commander to rack
Cell Number Two.

The electronic cell door buzzed as it rolled back.
The pair of C.O.'s quickly stepped to either side of
him and one knelt to attach the leg irons while the
other stood with his clipboard at his side and the
other hand resting on his gun butt.

Once the leg irons were in place, the C.O. rose,
carrying the handcuffs linked to lengths of chain. The
cuffs encircled his wrists and pinched off skin.

"Dammit," the squat C.O. muttered.

"What is it?" the other demanded.

"Just look at this guy's wrists. They're thick as
suspension cables. The cuffs don't fit."

"Make 'em fit."

Remo held his wrists out, his hands balled into
fists. The C.O. struggled to lock one cuff over his
right wrist. The tongue fell short of the locking mech-
anism by a half-inch.

"Try the other wrist," the tall C.O. said impatiently. "He's probably right-handed. The left wrist
will be thinner. And snap it up. The warden's waitin'."

The other handcuff also fell short of its task by a
good half-inch.

"What do we do?" the squat C.O. asked in exas-
peration. "I never saw a con with wrists like these."

Remo shot the guards a dark-eyed grin.

"What if I do this?" he suggested, unclenching his
fists.

The C.O. squeezed the cuffs. They clicked into
place.

"Cute," he said, giving Remo a shove. "Very cute.
Let's take your little magic act to the warden."

As he stepped from his cell, Remo was urged to
the right.

"Don't look back, boy. You don't want to see what's
back the other way."

A long row of cells stretched before him. Hands, some folded, others limp-fingered and bored, hung out the bars all along the line. The corridor was beige cinder block, and terminated in a black electronic door with a square glass window.

"Walk four steps behind me and hug the wall," the tall C.O. said, leading the way. The other one fell in behind them. "Stay on the yellow line."

Remo started walking heavily. As he passed the line of cells, hard unfamiliar faces peered out from between the green-painted bars.

"Hey, Sleeping Beauty! I'm Prince Charming."

"Say, what's your name, cutie?"

There were catcalls, a few wolf whistles. A washed-out con with a gold ring in his ear wondered aloud if Remo was a virgin. Remo stopped in front of his cell and fixed him with his dead-looking eyes. The con shrank back from the bars involuntarily.

Remo walked on, one second ahead of the trailing C.O.'s uncompleted shove.

As they were passed through a series of electronic doors and through a four-way intersection of floor-to-ceiling cell tiers, Remo asked a question.

"Where am I?"

"What do you mean?" the lead C.O. snarled. Then, recovering, he added, "That's right. You came in sedated, didn't you?"

"You tell me," Remo said as they came to the warden's office. The lead C.O. knocked on the door while they waited.

"Boy, your new home is the state penitentiary in Starke."

"My geography isn't so good," Remo said as the other C.O. poked his head into the door and announced, "He's here, sir."

"Florida," the other C.O. said flatly. "The land of sunshine and alligators."

"Don't forget Florida juice," the first guard added, pushing the door open for Remo.

Remo stepped into the warden's office, his chains dragging on the floor. His hands hung manacled below belt level, but his head was up, his posture defiant.

"Sit down, Williams," the warden said in a no-nonsense but unbelligerent tone of voice. He waved for the guards to shut the door behind them. Remo slipped into a simple wooden chair. The hard chair made him feel instantly uncomfortable. He wasn't sure why, but it stirred some vague, unreachable memory.

The warden made a point of ignoring Remo as he leafed through a manila file folder. He was a short, pugnacious man with a smooth bald head. There was a small pit in the flesh along the bridge of his nose, as if someone had chiseled a chunk out of it.

When the warden looked up, he let the folder fall flat. He gave it a last glance before turning his full attention to Remo.

"Do you know why you're here, Williams?"

"The state says I killed a drug pusher."

"That's why you were sent up to Trenton State Prison. I meant why you were transferred to Florida State."

Florida, Remo thought. So the guards weren't lying. Aloud he said, "It must have slipped my mind somehow." He wondered what the warden was talking about.

"You're a very foolish individual, Mr. Williams. You were better off back in New Jersey, where they don't take advantage of their death penalty. Up there, you were just another lifer on death row. But you kept getting into trouble. According to your sheet, you maimed your cellmate. Put out his eye over a cigarette. That was bad enough. But on top of that, you killed a guard. I imagine that guard had

family who had high political connections, because
someone pulled a lot of strings to get you transferred
to my prison. It's not legal, but when I protested, I
was told, in no uncertain terms, to play along. So I
am."

"Maybe I needed a change of scenery," Remo said
flatly. He wondered where this bullshit was going.

"You're pretty casual now," the warden resumed.
Remo noticed the nameplate in front of his desk said
he was Warden McSorley. "But I'm told the Trenton
officials had to sedate you for the transfer. So you
must know what you've gotten yourself into."

"Sure," Remo said coolly. "I got myself into
Florida."

"That's true," the warden said humorlessly. "But
you've also gotten yourself onto Florida's death row.
You see, unlike New Jersey, this state does take full
advantage of its death penalty. And since you've
been transferred into our jurisdiction, you fall under
Florida law."

Remo said nothing. His eyebrows drew together,
forming a deep notch.

"I'm sorry," the warden said in a voice that was
neither sympathetic nor sarcastic, but simply a voice.
"You were a police officer once, according to your
records. And I hold no truck with drug pushers.
Maybe you had your reasons for doing what you did,
but killing a corrections officer . . . well, my responsibility is to the law."

"I want to talk to my lawyer," Remo said tightly.

"I understand that an appeal has already been filed
on your behalf. In the meanwhile, you'll be expected
to obey the rules of this institution. You'll be allowed
out of your cell for two minutes every other day to
shower, and twice a week, on Mondays and Thurs-
days, for thirty minutes of supervised exercise in the
prison yard. Otherwise, you will be confined to your
cell, where you will take your meals and do all your

business. Given your rather extensive record of violence against corrections officers and fellow prisoners, I will have no choice but to put you into segregated detention if you misbehave in any way."

"You make me sound like a bad little boy," Remo said in a hard voice.

"Be assured, Mr. Williams, I do not see you in that light at all. Now, do you understand everything I have just told you?"

"Guess so."

"Do you understand what I mean by segregated detention?"

"Sure. Solitary."

"Is that what they call it up at Trenton?"

Remo had to think about that before answering.

"They called it administrative detention," he said at last.

"And I'm certain a man who's staring at the death penalty will think twice about living out his last days in solitary confinement." The warden pressed a buzzer. The two C.O.'s entered the room and took their places on either side of Remo Williams' unflinching face.

"Before these officers escort you back to your cell, do you have any questions?" the warden wanted to know.

Remo stood up, sending his chains clacking.

"Just one," he said quietly.

The warden looked up quizzically.

"Do you gas, inject, or fry in this state?"

"We have a very efficient electric chair, Mr. Williams. If it comes to that, you won't feel much more than a short-lived jolt. It's quite humane, really."

"Just the same, I think I'd prefer the needle."

The warden's face registered curious interest.

"Really?" he said. "If you don't mind my asking, why is that?"

"They don't shave your head before the lethal injection."

"Ah," the warden said as if understanding. But Remo could tell by the opacity in back of his eyes that he didn't understand at all.

Remo was silent as they led him away.

3

They waited until Remo was back in his cell before they removed the chains and leg irons. Remo sat on the bunk as the barred door clanged shut. For the first time he noticed the white sign fixed to the cell doors: DANGER! STAND CLEAR WHILE GATE IS IN MOTION in stark black death-warrant letters.

It was the only reading material in the cell, so Remo read it several times slowly.

A voice from the adjoining cell broke his concentration.

"Hey, Jim. What's happenin'?" The voice was black. Southern.

"The name's Remo."

"Don't be takin' no attitude, man. I calls all white boys Jim. What're you in for?"

"None of your business."

"Suit yourself. I was just bein' friendly. My name's Mohammed."

"In that case, my name's Allah."

"The Muslim brothers pronounces it Al-lah, whitey. But if it suits you, you can call me Popcorn. All the cons do. Just don't you be puttin' down my personal

god. Allah's all that be gettin' me through the day till
I gotta walk down the line. I killed my old lady,
don't you know."

"Tough."

"Don't I know it. Sometimes I really miss the
woman. Wouldn't have cut her, but I caught her in
bed with some turkey I never saw before. And it was
my birthday. That was the unforgiving thing, you
know."

"Spare me," Remo said, throwing himself back on
the cot. He stared up at the ceiling.

"I hear you was a cop once."

"Once," Remo said tonelessly.

"So what's a cop doin' in this empty place?"

"I forgot to Mirandize your mother."

"Hoo! You are some cold dude. But let me set you
straight, bro. The cons, they know you're a cop. The
hacks, they know you offed a guard. That put you
in a very bad place. I'd make all the friends I could
get, I was you."

"You're not me," Remo returned, suddenly wish-
ing for a cigarette. Maybe it would clear the cobwebs
from his mind. He felt like stale beer—flat and too
warm.

"In that case, I just got one more piece of advice
for you, Jim." When there was no answer, Popcorn
said, "Don't eat the meatloaf. It's always yesterday's
hamburger. And if they offer you meatloaf stew,
that's not only yesterday's meatloaf, it's also the day
before's hamburger. They don't waste shit in this
joint. They just reheat it and slide it back into your
sorry face all over again."

"I'll keep that in mind," Remo said, still staring at
the ceiling. It was too smooth. In his old cell, the
ceiling was cracked and peeling. He used to imagine
the cracks were an earthquake and the hanging flakes
volcanic eruptions. He used to follow the cracks with
his eyes for hours, imagining them—no, willing

them—wider. Sometimes, it seemed that they did widen, but they never widened enough to let him out, now matter how long he stared through the endless gray days and months.

Remo rolled to the side of his bunk. He found no entertainment in this flat unblemished ceiling. Staring at his shoes, he thought about what the warden had said.

He couldn't remember killing any guard back at Trenton State. But his mind was still fuzzy from sedation. Remo couldn't remember ever hearing of an inmate being shipped under sedation. Not a sane one. He wondered if he had cracked from the long years of imprisonment on death row.

He let his mind roll back over the years. It was all a flat gray blur. How many since the day they came for him at his Newark walk-up? Ten years? Twenty? Closer to twenty. Twenty long years since the judge— what was his name, Harold something?—had sent him up the river. In those days, New Jersey enforced its death penalty. Remo had sweated out over a year on death row—a "Dead Man" in the parlance of the other inmates—while his lawyer filed appeal after appeal.

It was not so much the appeals process that saved his life as it was the trend against invoking the death-penalty statutes that finally saved ex-patrolman Remo Williams' life. It wasn't vindication, but it was better than sitting on the chair.

Now, twenty years later, he was facing the chair all over again.

Remo stood up. His joints felt stiff. His not-quite-numb fingers stroked the stiff stubble of his chin and throat. There was no mirror in the cell. On death row a man might cheerfully slice open his throat rather than be dragged to the chair.

Swallowing reminded Remo of how dry his throat was. The washbasin was dry, so Remo decided to go in the other direction.

"I could use a smoke," he said aloud.

There was no answer from the left-hand cell, which Remo recalled had been empty when he passed it. But from the other side Popcorn asked, "Camel do for you?"

"Yeah."

"Well, here she come. One tailor-made."

Outside his cell door, a filterless cigarette rolled into view. Remo had to get down on his knees to snare it. But his wrists were too thick for the narrow space between the bars. He strained, his fingers nearly brushing the paper cylinder. He shifted to the other hand, but only succeeded in pushing the cigarette completely out of reach.

Remo returned to his bunk and sat down heavily, his face a mask of defeat.

After a while Popcorn remarked, "I don't smell no smoke, Jim. And I had my heart set on second-hand."

"It got away from me," Remo told him without emotion.

"That how I feel about my life, Jim. But you still owe me one."

"Sure," Remo said flatly. He felt like shit.

"Just don't be waiting long for payback. Sparky own my ass, you know."

"Who's Sparky? Your lawyer?" Remo wondered into the air. He might as well have been communicating with the dead. Popcorn's next words told him that he was.

"Sparky's the chair, man. I walk the line next month if my appeal don't stick. They tell you when you're going?"

"I'm not going," Remo said flatly.

"Do tell. I used to think that. The Man lets you think that for a while, him and his lawyers. After a while you get to believin' it yourself. Then they take it away from you an inch at a time. That's the bitch of it. One day you be flyin', the next you're scratchin'

in the dirt at your own damn feet, thinkin' that the
only way out is to dig your way out. But either way
you slice it, you be diggin' your own grave."

"I'm not going," Remo repeated.

"You figure 'cause you was once a cop, you got the
juice. That it?"

"They won't fry me. They didn't fry me in Jersey.
They won't fry me down here."

"Maybe so, Jim. But in this hole we in, Florida
juice got a whole 'nother meanin'. It ain't orange and
they gotta strap you down before you can get the
benefit of it."

"They can't transfer a man from one state to another and fry him. My lawyer will see to that."

"I'm with that. My lawyer's my last hope too."

"They won't fry me," Remo repeated. And suddenly he remembered why he had felt so uncomfortable sitting on the hardwood chair in the Warden's
office. Electric chairs were always built of noncon-
ducting wood.

A door buzzed down the passageway distantly.
Another buzzed. And each time, the buzzing was
louder as Control opened door after door. Then there
came the clear, unmuffled sound of footsteps.

The guards stopped outside Remo's cell. They were
the same guards as before.

"Today's shower day, Williams," one said, sneering.

Remo looked up from his bunk with dull eyes.

He stood up. "Why not?" he muttered.

This time they didn't cuff him as they brought him
out from the cell.

"Am I the only one who gets to wash off the dust?"
Remo asked.

The guard showed fierce teeth. "The others are
already getting nice and clean for you, Soap Boy.
Now, get moving."

Remo walked slowly past the range of death-row
cells. He met each glance in his direction boldly.

This time there were no catcalls or jeers. In a way, it was a bad sign.

They walked past the control booth at the prison crossroads, called Grand Central, where the watch commander buzzed them into the shower area. Remo stripped under the watchful eyes of the guards and stepped into the communal shower.

Dozens of pairs of hard eyes drank in his lean, tigerish muscles, his athlete-flat stomach and oddly thick wrists. Remo ignored them and stepped under the hot stream of an unoccupied shower head, lathering himself with a dirty bar of soap that stood melting in a gutterlike shelf that ran under the shower heads the entire length of the room. He rubbed some of the lather into his brown hair, scrubbed furiously, and, aware of the eyes on him, stepped back under the hot water until the last of the lather ran into the floor grates, to be carried away to the kind of freedom Remo hadn't known since he was half his current age.

As Remo started for the door, a man stepped in his path. He was white and built like a pregnant linebacker. His thick face was as expressionless as the Hoover Dam, except for the Fu Manchu mustache that had gone out of style when Gerald Ford was in the White House and a tiny dab of hair under his lower lip called a pachuco tuft. His black hair splayed all over his forehead, dripping dirty gray soap lather. He looked like a Klingon with a bad hairpiece.

"You the new Dead Man?" he growled.

"The name's Remo."

"Yeah. That's you. Dead Man," the man muttered as if Remo wasn't there. Then louder he said, "I hear you were a cop."

Remo said nothing. There was a phrase in the joint: Do your own time. It meant to mind your business and stay out of trouble. Remo decided he was going to follow it. He let his gaze drop to the man's soap-matted chest hair. Not in submission, but because the man was so much taller than Remo that Remo simply let his eyes rest at their natural level. He made his hard face still, betraying no emotion, neither weakness nor challenge.

"I used to eat cops," the man taunted.

"You tell 'im, McGurk," someone shouted.

McGurk leaned into Remo's face. His breath was sour. Like week-old buttermilk.

"Maybe I'll eat you." When Remo didn't reply, McGurk said, "Then again, maybe it'll be the other way around. I could protect you, cop. If you treat me right."

At that, Remo's gaze lifted. His eyes seemed to retreat into their deep sockets. Their expression was unreadable.

"You do for me and I'll do for you," McGurk said, low-voiced. "What d'you say?"

"I say," Remo said flatly, "that your breath smells like you've been sucking on an elephant's teat. Maybe you should stick with satisfying yourself that way."

McGurk's jaw dropped, making his pachuco tuft bristle.

The only sound in the room for a long time was the shower heads ejecting relentless streams of water.

Then a man released an explosive bark of a laugh. Another sucked in his breath. They moved in on Remo and the giant called McGurk to see what would happen next. Behind the big man, Remo could see the guards watching through the square window. Abruptly they turned their backs, and Remo knew there would be no help from them.

"All you swinging dicks stay out of this," McGurk said. He looked down at Remo. Remo met his gaze unflinchingly.

"I'll give you a choice, cop," McGurk said in a taut voice. "Your mouth on my jones right now or my shank in your gut."

"If you're packing, prove it," Remo said calmly.

McGurk spread out impossibly big hands and said, "No pockets, friend. But I'll get you in the yard."

"Then I'll see you in the yard," Remo said, pushing past the man and pulling open the door faster than McGurk could react.

Remo grabbed a towel off a rack and began drying himself as the obviously disappointed guards separated and took up positions by the outer door. The odor of stale sweat was a permanent stench in the room. The others drifted out, naked and sullen, and claimed their towels. When they were done, they threw the towels into a laundry cart and put on their clothes slowly, as if donning the blue state-issue dungarees made them less, not more, civilized.

As Remo reached for an identical uniform, one of the guards said, "No prison blues for you. Here."

Remo accepted an apricot-colored T-shirt. He pulled it over his head, and realized what it signified. Every man on the row had worn one. It was the badge of the condemned.

They formed a line, with Remo in the rear. The guards buzzed the door open and they walked out single file, their shoulders almost touching the right wall as they right-angled around corners until they passed the multiple-tier cellblocks surrounding Grand Central. The men ahead of Remo filed into their cells. They were general population. Remo continued on, alone, into the Q Wing, death row.

At a signal, the ranges of cell doors rolled open. The simultaneous clangor was deafening.

Remo walked toward the beige corridor to his open cell, just short of the last cell on death row.

A rough voice called after him, "In the yard, cop."

After the cell door buzzed shut with a temporary finality that Remo never got used to, he spoke a question into the air. "Know a con named McGurk?"

Popcorn's voice was wry. "Yeah. He's the dude

they call Crusher. Ain't that a comic-book name, man? Crusher McGurk. They say his first name's Delbert."

"Faggot?" Remo wondered.

"Yeah. Real butch. Why you ask? He take a shine to you?"

"Yeah."

"That Crusher, you gotta watch out for him. He pitches, but he don't catch. Know what I mean?"

"Yeah. He says he'll be looking for me in the yard."

"Then don't go into the yard."

"Have to. I have to keep in shape."

"What for? Ol' Sparky suck you dry in the end, bro."

"Someday I may get out of here," Remo said. He noticed that someone—himself or the guard—had kicked the corridor cigarette closer to the bars. He went over and put his hand through the bars. He forked the cigarette between two fingers and withdrew to his cot.

"Sure," Popcorn said as Remo examined the white paper for damage. It had split at one end and was dirty where a boot sole had crushed it. But the other end was clean. Remo flicked dust off it carefully. "Someday you'll get out," Popcorn was saying. "There's a white hearse that's gonna carry all us Dead Men outside of these walls one fine day. You can count on that."

"No. Not that way," Remo said, putting the clean end of the Camel into his mouth. "Someday they'll figure out that I'm innocent."

Remo ignored Popcorn's howling laughter as he searched his pockets for a match. He discovered he had no pockets, and of course there was no match either.

And Popcorn kept laughing as if Remo's innocence was the funniest thing on death row.

4

For Remo Williams, convicted murderer, his first day at Florida State Prison was not much different than all the days he could remember at Trenton State Prison. The guards came around for the ten o'clock head count. Lunch was served at twelve-thirty. Remo's food tray was placed on the shelflike slot in his cell door. It was meatloaf stew. He smelled it, and although he felt hungry, he returned the tray to the slot. By the time the guard came back to retrieve it an hour later, the surface had congealed into cold grease.

There was another head count at three in the afternoon, and again at eight. Lights-out came at the stroke of eleven, and a final bed check came twenty minutes later as a lone guard strolled down the line, pausing to turn his big D-cell flashlight on each cell. Once he called to a con to uncover his head. Only then did the beam pause for a moment; then its on-and-off activity continued.

The light came on in Remo's eyes and he turned over. The guard went on, repeated his ritual at Popcorn's cell, and then clumped away, his going punctuated by the diminishing loudness of the door buzzers as they closed in succession.

Remo stared at the flat blackness of his cell's outer wall, wondering if the nights here would be as bad as those in Trenton.

They were.

Distantly a voice called out, "Beam me up, Scotty," and Remo almost laughed. Except that the forlorn tone of the man's voice dampened the laughter. He had not been joking. In fact, he launched into an extended one-man performance of an imaginary *Star Trek* episode, playing in turn the parts of Captain Kirk, Spock, Scotty, McCoy, and even, in a ridiculous falsetto voice, Uhura.

"Shut your hole, chump!" a bass voice warned.

"You shut your hole. Let the man be. He be entertaining us."

That last came from Popcorn. Sighing, Remo rolled out of bed.

"Does this go on every night?" he asked.

"Some nights," Popcorn told him. "That be Radar Dish. He know every *Star Trek* episode by heart. Says he seen 'em seventeen times each. So naturally he get to the point where he roll his own, so to speak. You shoulda heard the one he spun last Saturday. When it was over, Kirk had got hisself zapped by the Romulans and Spock took over the bridge. First thing he do is to order retreat and start ballin' Uhura. That Radar Dish, he really gets into being Spock. But he likes to put his own spin on things."

Remo sighed. Back at Trenton, there had been a con who did *Dragnet* impersonations all night long. His Joe Friday had been so accurate that it prompted one lifer to stick a sharpened number-nine pencil into the con's Adam's apple, with fatal results. It seemed like a long time ago now. Remo couldn't even remember either man's name.

Finally the talking aloud, the sobbing, and the groaning tapered of and silence descended over the humid darkness of death row.

Remo slept.

In his sleep, he dreamed.

And in his dream, he was free.

Remo dreamed that he was riding an elevator to

the penthouse of a high-rise apartment building. He saw himself framed in the gold-wallpapered elevator cage, as if having an out-of-body experience. One hand was in his pocket and the other hung at his side, fingers snapping impatiently.

The elevator doors slid open and he started to step from the cage. He hesitated momentarily. The gleam that came into his eyes was short-lived. Then, casually taking the hand from his pocket, he stepped out into the corridor. He whistled.

From either side of the elevator doors, a burly man appeared. Each wore an expensive Italian silk suit. They carried compact little Mac-11 machine pistols. One placed the muzzle to Remo's neck and the other on his opposite side. Remo stopped whistling.

In his sleep he cried, "Oh, shit!" But in the dream he looked as cool as an actor starring in a TV movie of the week.

One of the two men mumbled, "Get off on the wrong floor, pal?"

To which Remo heard himself reply, "Not if this is Don Polipo Tentacolo's suite."

"Don Tentacolo ain't seeing visitors tonight, pal." This from the other man, the one who started patting Remo down. The other goon—there was no better word for him—kept his Mac-11 jammed in Remo's side.

What happened next happened so fast that it made Remo jerk in his sleep.

The kneeling guard was checking Remo's ankles when one of Remo's feet snapped up. The toe seemed only to tap the man's chin, but his head flew back like it was on the end of a snapped cable. The crack of splintering vertebrae was as distinct as thunder.

Then—or perhaps it occurred simultaneously, because Remo's attention was on the head snapping back and not elsewhere—the dream Remo twisted his upper body so that the pistol muzzle pointed at thin air. He took the other goon by the wrist. Instead of exerting pressure against the natural flex point of the joint as he'd been taught at the police academy, Remo inserted his pinky finger into the open muzzle of the Mac-11. The sound of the barrel splitting merged with the crack of the splintering vertebrae.

The Mac-11 fell apart as if every weld and screw had simultaneously disintegrated, leaving the goon holding a very shaky gun butt with the shiny little bullets visible in the exposed top of the magazine clip.

The goon looked down at his useless weapon and then at his fallen comrade, whom Remo dislodged from his expensive Italian loafers with a casual flick of his ankle.

"May I?" Remo asked, smiling politely. And without waiting, he extracted a bullet from the clip. Another bullet sprang up to replace it.

Remo watched himself take the tiny bullet in one hand and place it against the goon's forehead. Then, with coiled forefinger, he tapped the primer cap on the end of the shell casing. There came a firecracker *pop*! and the standing goon suddenly became the prone dead goon with a black crater in the center of his forehead.

Remo casually stepped over the bodies and walked up to a black door of fine wood. He knocked on the door and waited, hands on hips.

In his cell, Remo tossed in his sleep. He noticed for the first time how thin his arms were. He looked like he had lost all his natural body fat and thirty percent of his musculature. His wrists, however, were unusually thick. The combination made him think of Popeye the Sailor Man—but less grotesque.

Remo was staring at his own oddly expanded wrists when a splintery hole jumped into the black door panel and his dream self simply faded back from the

line of fire—for the solitary hole had been made by a
gun pressed to the opposite side of the door.

The dream Remo lunged forward, the palm of his
hand striking the doorknob with such force that it
shot from its socket and into the penthouse. An
unseen man howled in exquisite agony, and Remo
casually pushed the door open.

He paused beside a man holding his groin with
both hands in a doubled-up stance only long enough
to poke him in the eyes. Before he fell face-forward,
Remo caught a glimpse of the mashed jelly his eye
sockets now contained. If he hadn't been sleeping,
he would have turned away.

In the dream, Remo was moving from room to
room in an elegant penthouse suite until he found a
man cowering against a plate-glass window that gave
him a panoramic view of some unidentified city.
There was neon piping in the background. It was not
rolled into scroll or signwork, but edged several tall
office buildings. That told Remo that the penthouse
overlooked Dallas, Texas.

The fat man had his back to the glass as if he were
standing on a narrow ledge and only the friction of
the glass kept him from falling to his death.

"If you're a cop," he was saying, "I can pay you."

"Wrong guess," Remo heard himself say.

"If you're a fed, I can roll over."

"Not even close."

"Then what do you want?"

"Oh, a nice home, a pleasant wife, maybe a couple
of kids."

"Done! I'll set it up." The fat man was sweating,
even though he outweighed Remo by an easy sixty
pounds.

"Sorry," Remo told him. "There are some things
not even money can buy. It won't buy me, and it
won't buy the life I want."

"There's gotta be something we can do," Don Tentacolo said urgently. "Some deal we can cut."

"Let me think about this," Remo said disinterestedly. He tapped the glass beside the man's head. The fat man winced as if Remo's fingers were hypodermics.

"Is this a single pane or a sandwich?" Remo asked.

"Single. Bulletproof."

"Good," said Remo, tracing a ruler-straight line over the fat man's quaking head. The glass squealed as if scored by a glass cutter. Then Remo ran the finger from one end of the line to the floor and repeated the action on the other side.

The manipulation framed the fat man in a thin white rectangular line, rather like the outline of a coffin.

"What . . . what are you going to do?" he quavered.

"You look hot. Like you could use some air."

"Yeah," Don Tentacolo said, wiping his forehead. "It's roasting in here."

"Then permit me," Remo said. He placed his hand on the man's heaving chest and gave him what looked like a gentle shove.

Except that there was nothing gentle about the way Don Polipo Tentacolo went through the thick glass, taking with him a doorlike rectangle of glass. His feet were the last things to disappear into the darkness beyond the window.

Remo saw himself lean out of the opening in the glass, and his dream viewpoint suddenly dollied to follow the madly gesticulating body as it fell twenty or thirty stories to the hard pavement below.

The glass struck first. It shattered into thousands of separating shards. The fat man shattered too, but the bag that was his fleshy envelope kept his disintegrating bone structure from becoming organic shrapnel.

With one notable exception. A short length of

femur shot out of his trouser seam to impale his left palm.

Dusting off his hands as if having completed a minor but stubborn household-repair task, Remo's dream self turned from the window as if to go. But recognition crossed his face and he gave a cocky half-grin and asked an unseen person, "How did I do?"

The responding voice was squeaky and querulous, like Daffy Duck after a hard day on the set.

"Your elbow was bent," it said bitterly.

And the expression of disapointment that spread over Remo's dream face was tragic.

Remo woke up with the identical expression on his true face. He just didn't know it.

Popcorn's voice whispered through the shell-pink cinder block to his ear, "You okay, Jim?"

Remo sat up. "Had a bad dream," he said quietly.

"Got news for you. You still havin' it. 'Cept now your eyes are open. You dig me?"

"I know where I am. It just seemed so real." And for the first time, Remo's voice had lost the hard edge that prison life had made second nature.

"I got a sayin', Jim: Dead Men dream deepest. You be on death row awhile, you get to know what I'm sayin'."

Remo felt under his pillow. The Camel was still there, only now it had developed a fissure and resembled a bent paper nail.

"Don't suppose you have a match?" Remo prompted.

"Not since Muhammad Ali went soft in the head."

"That's old."

"In stir, every joke is old. If I slip you a matchbook, you gonna slide it back afterward?"

"Sure."

"Okay, my man. Don't screw up any worse than you did to get here."

The matchbook slid into view like a dim hockey puck. It came to rest beside a cell bar and Remo retrieved it on the first try. He tore off a match and struck it. The flame caught the dirty end of the Camel in Remo's mouth.

Remo sat on his bunk and took a deep drag.

The tobacco smoke hit his lungs like mustard gas. The urge to cough was overpowering. He tried to choke it back, knowing that it could bring the guards or, worse, wake up every man on death row. But the coughing refused to be suppressed.

Remo went to his knees. He put his head under the cot and surrendered to a coughing fit. He hacked like a twelve-year-old trying to get through his first smoke.

"You okay, Jim?" Popcorn hissed. "You gonna bring down all kinds of shit on our sorry heads if you don't stifle yourself."

Remo's coughing spasms trailed off into a strangled moan.

"Don't you die on me, Jim," Popcorn pleaded. "You got my last book a' matches. Don't you die on me."

Through his own pain Remo heard the sincerity in Popcorn's voice. Prison sentimentality. Don't die until I get back what's mine. He never got used to its callous ruthlessness.

Finally Remo crawled back into his bunk.

"First time?" Popcorn asked wryly.

"I'm used to filtered cigarettes," Remo said. His lungs felt like they were on fire. Instead of clearing his head, the nicotine dulled his brain even more. Maybe, he thought, he was having a reaction to the sedative that had kept him asleep during the trip from New Jersey. Still, he shouldn't have a reaction like that. He was a pack-a-day man.

"What about my matches, man?"

"In the morning," Remo shot back weakly. "I'm sick."

"You crazy if you think you're gonna keep my matches, sucker," Popcorn hissed. "You hear me?" The speed with which Popcorn's easy solicitude had turned hard and then nasty was elemental.

Remo turned over and tried to find sleep, but it eluded him until the five-o'clock buzzer, and then, too soon, it was the start of another interminable gray day.

5

Before the guard appeared with the breakfast trays, Remo set the matchbook outside the bars of his cell and gave it a single-finger shove.

"There it is," he called. "Got it?"

"Yeah, man, I got it." Popcorn's voice was wary. Remo imagined him opening up the cover to carefully count each match. He must have done it twice because it was a while before his voice, again suffused with cocky good humor, came back.

"That's two you owe me, Jim," he said. "One for the tailor-made and the other for the igniter."

"Catch you in the yard sometime," Remo said.

"If we get the yard on the same day."

Breakfast was cold cornflakes in a single-serving package and a separate pint container of low-fat milk. Remo poured the milk over the flakes slowly. The smell of it was strong. He put his nose to the bowl. Not sour. Just strong. He had never smelled milk this strong. Funny. He had never thought of fresh milk as having a smell before.

Remo decided to skip the sugar and forced the first spoonful down his throat. It went down hard. The flakes felt like they were sandpapering his esophagus. He got it down. Five minutes later he threw it up all over the floor.

"You sure you done time before, Jim?" Popcorn's voice was wary again. "You don't seem to be acclimatizin' none too good. Hate to think you was a fish. 'Cause if you was a fish, that'd mean you was a rat. Though what the Man would be doing puttin' a rat on the row is more than I can understand."

"You got anything to rat about?" Remo asked, spitting the last of the milk from his mouth. It tasted sour now, but that was stomach-acid taste.

"No. But you be acting like a first-timer, not a lifer."

"I haven't smelled free air since . . ." Remo hesitated. When did he go in first? Was in '71. No, earlier, '70. Maybe '69. No, it couldn't have been '69. He remembered pounding a beat in '69, just another beat cop on his way to a faraway pension.

The C.O. came around for the tray and saw the mess on Remo's floor. His tight expression turned into a glower.

"You do that on purpose?" he demanded hotly.

"I threw up," Remo told him.

The guard looked closer. "Doesn't look like vomit to me."

"It wasn't in my stomach more than two minutes," Remo said with the sullenness that came to a prisoner after being in the joint for so long that all the pride had seeped out of the soul. It was a consequence of being treated, for all intents and purposes, like a dangerous teenager.

Popcorn spoke up. "I can vouch for whitey, there,"

he said. "I heard him throw. Man sounded like he
was coughin' up his lungs. Kidneys too."

"Shut up, Dead Man."

The guard went away, coming back with a mop
and bucket.

"Rack Number Two," he called down the line. The
door to Remo's cell rolled aside. The C.O. shoved
the mop and bucket in through the half-open door.

"Clean it up," he told Remo.

Remo looked in the bucket and said, "No water."

"Boy, you got endless water," the guard said, pointing to the open stainless-steel toilet.

Remo dipped the mop into the open bowl, slopped
it into the bucket, and carried both over to the mess.
He swabbed the floor until it was clean, emptied the
bucket into the bowl, and then brought bucket and
mop back to the cell door.

"Wring it out first," the guard insisted.

"With what?" Remo demanded.

"You got hands."

"I don't shower again until tomorrow."

"I don't make the rules," the guard said. "I just
enforce them. Maybe next time you feel like puking,
you'll try harder to hold it down."

Scowling, Remo wrung out the mop with his bare
hands and emptied the bucket into the toilet bowl.

The guard took the mop and bucket and locked
the door. He called down the line, "Rack Number
One." He stepped up to the next cell, beyond Remo's
sight. "Okay, Popcorn, time to hose down your poor
black ass."

"You just saying that 'cause you love me," Popcorn
told the guard.

The door buzzed open, and Remo, holding his
dripping hands in front of him, looked up with sudden interest.

He got a shock. The man who sauntered by, flashing him an easy Ipana smile, was short and reedy,

wearing a high-top fade haircut that made his head look like a well-used pencil eraser. He was not much more than eighteen.

"How ya doing, Jim?" he said, and just as quickly was gone.

"Damn," Remo muttered. "Just a kid. He's just a kid."

After the ten-o'clock check, Remo was told it was his day to exercise in the yard. Popcorn had long since returned to his cell.

The cell door buzzed open and Remo stepped out. There beside him was Mohammed, alias Popcorn.

"Looks like we go together," the little con remarked.

"Looks like," Remo said.

"No talking in line," the guard snapped. It was a different guard than the man who had forced Remo to wring his acid-and-milk breakfast from the mop. By this time Remo's hands had dried to a milky tightness. He had gotten so sick of the smell that he had, after flushing the toilet six or seven times consecutively, washed his hands in the bowl. It was degrading, but no more so than any of the other indignities that had happened to him over the last two decades.

They walked down death row, where the apricot-T-shirted inmates regarded them with unblinking serpentlike eyes to C Block. One long-haired blond man sat on the bottom of his bunk—they had bunk beds in C Block—his eyes blank, his head swiveling from side to side like a human radar dish.

"That be Radar Dish," Popcorn whispered to Remo. "They say he ate his mother. He be one fucked-up dude."

High up on the second tier of cells that made up C Block, a gravelly voice sang out. "In the yard," it warned.

"And you know who that be," Popcorn said. "Del-

bert himself. AKA the Crusher." Popcorn pronounced
the nickname with evident relish, extending the last
syllable as if tasting it.

"McGurk carry a shank?" Remo asked. The C.O.
grumbled at them, but didn't interfere with the
conversation.

"Some days," Popcorn supplied. "But Delbert, he
don't need no shank, you see. Heard it said of him he
once cornered a man he like in the machine shop
and pinned him to the wall. Planted a big wet one on
the dude's mouth. Man fight back, as is natural with
a man. Delbert, he don't like that. He want a piece
of you, he figure that be his right. So he pry open
that man's jaw with his thumbs and take hold of the
dude's tongue with his teeth. Bit down hard, did my
man Delbert. Took half of his tongue. Swallowed it
like raw liver. Then he held that poor suffering bastard's face down on the floor until he done bleed to
death. Leastways, that's the way I heard it told."

Remo grunted. He wondered if Popcorn was trying
to scare him. Some cons took pleasure in testing a
newcomer's nerve.

But Remo Williams was no newcomer. He had
done hard time. He was afraid, but he wasn't frightened. That slim distinction often was the margin by
which a man survived imprisonment.

They passed through the last door to the yard. It
was empty.

Remo relaxed. Then Popcorn spoke up. "Don't get
comfortable," he said. "The row always get first
crack at the yard before they turn the population
loose."

And behind them, the cacophony of buzzers indicated that C Block was being released from their
cages. They milled out like schoolkids at recess, everyone talking but no single voice rising above any other.

"Catch you later," Popcorn said, edging away from
Remo. "If you live."

Remo hung back near a corner of the yard. The institution was a lime-green building surrounded by a double Cyclone fence. Green watchtowers thrust up in battlementlike extensions by the fence. The sun was high and it was warm, but muggy, as if they were near the ocean. Remo could almost smell the salt air.

The cons came out like a human wave, but quickly separated into groups. Cellies paired off or split up, each according to the tension of the day. The lames— those who couldn't adjust to prison life—went off by themselves. The obvious queens gathered together, talking in high-pitched voices. A basketball game started under a single forlorn hoop.

And towering above even the tallest of the general population was the bullet head of Crusher McGurk. His eyes, small and mean and overhung by bony brows, sought out Remo.

Remo met the giant's gaze with frank contempt.

Crusher pushed a pair of squealing queens apart and started out of the crowd. Instead of coming toward Remo, however, he made a bounding, belly-swaying beeline for Popcorn, who stood with his back to the population, shading his eyes from the overhead sun. His head was tilted back. He was watching a lone sea gull wheeling in long lazy circles just over the north fence.

He didn't see or hear Crusher come up on him with the steady flat-footed walk of a man who didn't care where he stepped or what he stepped in—or on. It was obviously all the same to Crusher McGurk.

One of Crusher's big hammy paws lifted up and snared the top of Popcorn's hairdo and twisted his head around sharply. Popcorn spun with the twist, almost losing his footing.

"What you on me for, man?" Popcorn said, his voice skittering into a high fearful wail. One second his face was dry, the next it looked as if it had been smeared with oil. That's how quickly the sweat oozed from his pores. "Leggo my 'do!"

McGurk's growled response was too low for Remo to catch. He debated his best move. He decided to simply get this over with.

He walked up behind McGurk.

"Let him go," Remo said coldly.

McGurk, not letting go, twisted his face around. A fierce expression crept over it.

"Is this your wife come to rescue you, Popcorn?" McGurk growled, lifting Popcorn's elastic scalp. "Or maybe it's the other way around."

"I barely know the dude, Crusher," Popcorn insisted.

"I said let him go," Remo repeated, then adding tightly, "Delbert."

"Crusher's my street name, motherfucker."

"And Delbert's the name your mother gave you. She had you pegged better than the street."

Crusher McGurk's expression was momentarily stupefied. His bristling brows dropped lower over his eyes. They narrowed so tightly that they started to cross.

Crusher muscled Popcorn around in front of him and gathered him into a headlock. Popcorn, his face dripping perspiration now, simply extended his hands in abject surrender.

Crusher squeezed. Popcorn's face darkened almost immediately.

"Look at me," Crusher taunted. "I'm making the nigger turn colors. Hey, cop. Ever seen a nigger choke? First he gets darker, then he goes kinda purple. White folks turn blue. Not a nigger. They favor purple. Even the tongue goes purple. Show the man, nigger."

Crusher squeezed and Popcorn gagged. His tongue lolled out of his mouth. He began making strangling, hacking sounds. Popcorn's tongue was pink. But his lips were turning faintly purple.

"Oooh, look at that long lapping tongue," Crusher said. "No wonder you don't want no harm coming to this homeboy. I'll bet he gives head almost as good as you, cop."

"The name is Remo," Remo said, taking a step forward. "McJerk."

Crusher split his lips in a bestial grin. Abruptly he released Popcorn. The wiry black teenager fell to his knees, clutching his throat with one hand and supporting himself with the other.

"Now I know what you care about," McGurk said hotly, "I'll give you time to think my offer over. You become my slave, or next time the nigger turns purple. Forever. Next time. In the yard."

And Crusher swaggered away into the population. The other cons gave him a wide berth.

Remo offered Popcorn his hand. It was a minute before Popcorn was conscious of it. He accepted the gesture and let Remo help him to his feet.

"Don't know whether to be thankin' you or blamin' you," Popcorn muttered. "So if it's just the same, I'll do neither."

Remo looked up at the guard towers. Their windows were smoked glass.

"Don't the hacks try to break up fights?" he asked.

"Sometimes. But they be afraid of Delbert too. Delbert, he take on anyone. Guard or con, it don't matter to him. He feels the same way about sex. A mouth is a mouth to Delbert. A man's asshole is just as snug as a woman's. Besides, man, you offed a guard up in Jersey. Everybody know that. So don't be looking to the hacks for no help."

"I don't remember killing any guard in Jersey or anywhere."

"Say it again for luck," Popcorn said. "Amnesia get me through most nights too."

Before Remo could say another word, Popcorn sauntered off. Remo let him go. He was staring into

the guard towers. He felt eyes on him. For all he
knew, the guards were sighting on him down their
telescopic rifle sights. They used to do that back at
the other prison. Just for practice. Only there you
could see them. Remo didn't like the smoked glass.
He preferred to look his tormentors in the eye.

He shrugged and dropped to his hands and toes.
He started with push-ups, then went into a flurry of
leg lifts, with the right and then the left leg, revers-
ing and doing equal numbers of reps. On death row
he'd have no access to the weight room—assuming
Florida State Prison even had a weight room—so he
had to make the best of his opportunitites to maintain
his physique.

While he exercised, Remo checked out the yard.
It was set in what seemed to be the northeast corner
of the prison. Remo could see the front gate from his
vantage point. The tall Cyclone fence was broken by
a section of chain-link gate that moved on rollers.
The gate section was taller than the main fence by a
good three feet. Beyond it was a lime-green gatehouse that looked like one of the watchtowers had
given birth to an infant correctional outhouse. The
razor wire atop the fencing was strung in wide loops.
It wasn't electrified. That meant that the best way
out was over the wall and past the guard towers. It
was hardly an option, not with the guards invisible
behind smoked glass; there was no way to tell when
they were looking in an escapee's direction and when
they were not.

The buzzer announced an end to yard time, and
Remo, not in a hurry, leisurely drifted back toward
the main building.

At the entrance, a guard stopped him with a white
nightstick against his chest. It was the squat C.O.
who had manacled him the day before.

"You," he said gruffly. "Dead Man. Step out of line."

Woodenly Remo stepped out and took his place against the wall.

"Strip and spread 'em, boy."

"I didn't do anything," Remo protested.

"Not yet. Not here. But where you come from, you shanked a guard. I'm gonna see that you don't shank me while you're in sunny Florida. Now, strip and spread your cheeks."

Remo hesitated. To refuse would mean to go on report. Probably go to solitary. No more yard time.

Remo was considering if it was worth it, when the captain of the guards strolled out and pointed to the guard who had Remo.

"You!" he barked. "Pepone. Find Mohammed Diladay and bring him to interrogation."

"Once I'm done with this one," Pepone shot back.

"No. Now." The captain of the guards stormed off.

The guard's face fell. He placed his hand on Remo's shoulder and walked him back into the marching line.

"Next time," he whispered in Remo's ear. "Boy."

Remo said nothing. He kept walking. He was a marked man now, and he knew it. The guards were out to get him—if McGurk didn't get him first. Solitary started to look good.

Remo watched the guard named Pepone move along the line until he found Popcorn and pulled him out. Mohammed went along with more of the usual bounce to his step. Remo wondered where he was going and if it had anything to do with the altercation in the yard.

An hour later, another C.O. brought Popcorn back to his cell. He walked with his head down and his eyes on the yellow line. If he was aware of Remo, he gave no sign as he passed Remo's cell. Taking the hint, Remo left him in peace. He would open up in time.

It was after the dinner trays had been collected that Popcorn finally made a sound. He didn't speak. Instead he broke down into an inarticulate sob and went on for ten racking minutes before his animallike grunting broke into a long wail of despair.

Remo waited until he fell silent and asked quietly, "Want to talk about it?"

"I talked to my mouthpiece, man," Popcorn sniffled. "They turned down my last appeal. I go Tuesday. Tuesday! You'd think they'd give a poor black man a month to get his shit together. Or a week. I'd settle for a week. But I cook on Tuesday."

"Tough," Remo said. The hardness in his voice belied his sympathy. Popcorn had reverted from the cellwise con he pretended to be to what he truly was—a poor dumb teenager who had screwed up on his birthday and was about to pay for it with his life.

"What do they think this is?" Popcorn demanded of the walls. "China? What did I do that was so bad? Sure, I killed her. But who's to know she wouldn't have died of cancer by now anyway. Smoked like a chimney, that woman did. I may have done her a favor by doin' her quick. Yeah, that's it, I did her a favor, poor bitch. But jeez, man, I don't wanna fry."

"I heard it's painless," Remo said hollowly.

"You heard shit, man," Popcorn said vehemently. "Five dudes have gone since I come here. The Man say it don't hurt, but how do they know? They ain't sat there themselves. Ain't no one who sat on ol' Sparky ever came back to say, 'Shit, man, it's a cakewalk. Best way to go.' You know what they do, Jim?"

"Yeah," Remo said, surprised that his earlier craving for a cigarette hadn't returned. "I know."

"They strap you in so tight that if they rammed a red-hot poker up your ass, you couldn't even squirm. They hook you up forehead, leg, and jones. Put a veil over your face to deny a last look at the world. It be cold, man. Cold. Then they zap you. If you be lucky, you cook fast. I hear of suckers who had to drink Florida juice twice before the eyes turn white. The electricity, you know, it cooks the eyeballs white. You die like a blind man. There's nothing lower, not even a dog dies so cruel. Oh, Jesus. Why me?"

"Jesus? What happened to Allah?" Remo blurted out.

"That was for the brothers' benefit. I die Tuesday. Jesus is my savior now. Only I don't think he can save me now."

Remo shuddered. Neither of them said another word for the rest of the night. After lights-out, the row fell silent, as if out of respect for the condemned man whose cell would be empty in a few days.

That night, Remo dreamed again.

In the dream, they came for him in the middle of the night. A monk came first. He had only one hand and offered his crucifix for Remo to kiss. Remo sank to his knees and obliged.

Then they walked him down the line. Remo was surprised, even in sleep, that the corridor was of cold gray stone. It wasn't Florida. It was Trenton. They strapped him in so tight he could barely breathe. Instead of a veil, they put a leather hood over his head. It was as heavy as a medieval torture device. Then they clamped the copper helmet over his head and screwed the electrode until it touched his sweaty temple. He already felt the coldness of the electrode at his leg, where it was affixed through the split in his trouser leg. He knew that coldness would snap suddenly into a red-hot bite when the switch was pulled by the executioner.

Even though there were no eye holes in the leather, Remo could see the executioner—a short nonde-script man with a solemn face. He could see him

reach for the switch. The switch came down and
Remo's brain exploded into a white burst of light.
His body jerked against the straps and in his mouth
was an acrid taste as he bit down on something—
something that he had been careful to keep under
his tongue. . . .

He couldn't remember what it was.

Remo snapped awake in the middle of the night.
He could hear Popcorn's irregular breathing. Once
the rhythms of his exhalations stopped, and resumed
only after he let out a gusty sigh. Remo decided to
leave him alone with his thoughts.

He had his own thoughts to think. The dream had
seemed so real, just like the one of the previous
night. But it was equally preposterous. Remo thought
it was interesting that in the dream he had been
executed at Trenton State. But then he remembered
that at Trenton he used to dream of being in his
Newark walk-up. And before that, when he was a
free man, his dreams always took him back to the
orphanage where he was raised, Saint Theresa's.

It struck Remo that his dreams were always behind
the times. And he wondered forlornly if he would
ever see a time when he would dream of being in
Florida State Prison, and where he would be when
that happened.

Eventually he drifted off. This time, he did not
dream. . . .

6

Remo awoke before the morning buzzer. Groggily he rolled out of his cot. To his surprise, in the next cell, Popcorn was belting out an old fifties doo-wop song, "Desiree," performing the lead vocals, harmony, and "wah-wah" accompaniment not quite simultaneously, but close enough to be music.

"You okay?" Remo asked during the final fading "Oooo Oooo."

"Sure," Popcorn sang. "I got it all figured out now."

"Yeah?"

"The state taketh and the state giveth away," Popcorn said archly, and burst out laughing.

"Glad you're taking it so well," Remo grunted, joining in the macabre mood.

"Sure, I ain't gonna die cooking on Sparky's frypan."

"No?"

"Crusher's gonna get me first, Jim. Told you I got it all figured out. He done threatened to kill me if you don't go down on him. So come yard time, you let him break my neck. You show him you ain't afraid of nothing. Maybe he let you be."

"You'll still be dead," Remo pointed out.

Popcorn snorted explosively. "A day early and a dollar short," he admitted. "But at least my death will count for something. It don't mean shit if I die sitting with state ghouls gettin' off the smoke pourin' out my shoes, mouth, and armpits."

"Thanks," Remo said tonelessly, wondering if he meant it.

"Don't thank me. Thank my grinnin' corpse," Popcorn shot back. "Maybe I'll take ol' Crusher with me and do everyone a favor. A man with nothing to lose can do most everything. 'Cept live."

"I heard that," Remo said tightly.

Breakfast was runny eggs and fat strips with the shadow of bacon meat on them. The bacon was cold by the time it reached Remo, and the smell of it nearly turned his stomach—as if it were cooked human flesh. There was a pint carton of orange juice and Remo tried that. It seared his tongue to taste and burned his throat going down. But it stayed down. He ignored everything else.

Today was shower day and Remo lay on his bunk waiting for the guards. He was getting tired of staring at the flat ceiling so he sat up and transferred his attention to the pink cinder-block walls.

"Hey, Popcorn," he called.

"Yo."

"What color are your walls?"

"Same as yours. Pink as quiff."

"I hate pink."

"A hack once told me they painted every cell on the row pink to keep us poor Dead Men down. Scientist dudes think pink keeps our aggressions pacified. Makes pussies of us."

"You've been here awhile. Does it work?"

"Well," Popcorn said sadly after a lengthy pause, "I can't tell you the last time I got it up and kept it there."

Remo laughed out loud. When Popcorn didn't join in, Remo realized the little con had taken offense and was sulking. Remo decided to let him get over the mood on his own.

When the guards came, Remo knew at once that they had not come to escort him to the shower room.

Although he had no watch, and no window in his cell, he sensed it was too early for his shower. Only after they let him from his cell and walked him down the longest death row in the country did it dawn on him that no one else was going to a shower either.

"What's this, Adopt-a-Con week?" Remo asked, looking neither right nor left at the flanking C.O.s.

"Your lawyer's here," one growled.

Remo's eyebrows lifted in surprise, but he said nothing.

As they approached the inmate-choked prison crossroads, the other guard called out, "Clear the hall! Dead Man walking! Clear the hall!"

Instantly, denim-clad population inmates returned to their cells or gave way like human traffic before a fire engine. Remo felt like a leper. It had not been like this up in Jersey, but then, no one on the Trenton State death row expected to be executed.

After they had passed, the human sea surged back into place. Remo felt countless eyes on him. He saw no sign of Crusher McGurk.

Near the warden's office, protected by bars of specialty steel, was a suite of conference rooms and outside of it a bright yellow cage. Not a cell. It was like an animal's cage.

Remo was placed in this. He took a seat on a hardwood bench and waited. The hours passed before a guard came and opened the cage. It was the squat one who had tired to strip-search Remo the day before. Pepone. He gave Remo a wolfish grin.

"Looks like I get to finish what was interrupted yesterday," he said. "Now, strip."

This time Remo didn't hesitate. If he resisted normal previsitation procedure, he would be denied all visitation rights and not see his lawyer. And if Pepone wrote up a report on him, he'd end up in solitary and probably never see his lawyer.

Remo wanted to see his lawyer. And so quietly he removed his apricot T-shirt and dungarees.

"Now drop your drawers, spread your cheeks, and crack a smile," Pepone said.

Remo hesitated. Some spark flickered in his still-groggy mind. He looked Pepone straight in the eye and said, "I'm not carrying any contraband. Take my word for it."

Pepone's broad face darkened. "Think about it, Williams. It's just you and me in this cage. No way out."

"For either of us," Remo said, putting cold meaning into the pronoun.

"You know the rules of this facility."

"And you know my reputation," Remo countered.

Pepone stiffened. He looked around. There were no other guards nearby. "Okay," he said dully. "Dress."

Remo dressed quickly, and only then was he led into one of the conference rooms.

There was only one other person in the room, a curly-haired young man who sat nervously on one side of the glass-partitioned conference cubicle. Remo strode up to the cubicle and took the seat. He fixed the man with his deep eyes. "You're not my lawyer," he said suspiciously.

"I'm local. Mr. Brooks asked me to manage your appeal through the Florida court system, now that you're under their jurisdiction. My name is George Proctor."

"I didn't hire you. I hired Brooks," Remo said flatly.

"In all fairness to Mr. Brooks, he doesn't know his way around the Florida courts. I do. And you can't expect him to fly down here every time your appeal goes before a judge, can you?"

Remo said nothing. He didn't know this man. He looked fresh out of Tulane. Worse, he looked nervous. And nervous men usually don't have the presence of mind to do the right thing in a crunch.

"Are we clear on this, Mr. Williams?" Attorney Barry Proctor was saying.

"Where do I stand?" Remo asked at last.

Proctor took a sheaf of legal briefs out of his flat leather valise and looked them over. It seemed to Remo as if he were looking at them for the first time. Another bad sign.

"Florida isn't New Jersey, Mr. Williams," Proctor said at last. "We have the largest death row in the country, and space is at a premium. They process people through the system as fast as they can."

"They execute them, you mean."

"Er, yes. That's what I mean. Because we're in a new state and a fresh legal system, I thought we'd start from scratch."

"The last I heard, my case would be appealed to the Supreme Court," Remo offered.

"Frankly, Mr. Williams, according to Brooks, he's been carrying you these last few years. Your life savings have been exhausted. Now, don't get me wrong. I'm willing to go through the appeals court in Miami on the grounds that having been transferred against your will to another state, you're entitled to at second bite of the judicial apple."

"I'm innocent," Remo said.

"The New Jersey authorities claim you killed one of their corrections officers."

Remo paused. His eyes went blank. It was starting to come back. The constant hassling. The whispered threats. And the fight in the cell. He saw the hack's weather-beaten face go shocked as the blade dug into his guts. "He was riding me," Remo said. "He wouldn't get off my back. It was either him or me."

"Then you admit to killing him."

"Remo sighed. "Yeah," he said in a defeated voice. "I did the guard. But not the pusher in the alley. I was framed for that one." As soon as the words were out of his mouth, Remo realized what he sounded like.

He sounded exactly like every other whiny con on the row.

"You know what I think?" Proctor was saying. "I think New Jersey dumped you on Florida to save themselves the cost of a new trial for that killing. They knew you would never be executed up there, no matter how many guards you killed. But in Florida you have an excellent chance of going to the chair within the next five years."

"Can they do that? Legally, I mean."

"It's highly unusual," Proctor admitted. "Frankly, I think the fix is in on you."

"They're trying to railroad me," Remo said bitterly. But his eyes were bleak. It was starting to sink in. After all these years, he might actually pay for a crime he never committed because of another killing that wouldn't have happened if he hadn't been wrongly imprisoned.

Proctor shoved the papers back into his valise.

"I'll do what I can," he said, starting to offer his hand in a farewell shake. His manicured fingernails tapped the glass partition and he withdrew the hand sheepishly.

Proctor stood up and signaled to the guard. A C.O. took Remo away, again calling, "Clear the hall! Dead Man coming through!" over and over until Remo began to feel very cold inside.

Half the cells on death row were empty as Remo made his way through the endless succession of control doors to his cell. He had missed his shower. And for the first time, he realized the significance of the black door which sealed off the corridor two cells down from his own cell. Beyond it was the electric chair.

Remo felt drained after the cell door buzzed closed and the guard had departed.

He paced the cell, feeling the craving for a cigarette return. But he remembered his last experience. What was wrong with him? he wondered. He was acting like a fish—a man new to prison. It must have been the sudden change in environment, he decided. The last thing he remembered was going to sleep in his old cell. They must have sedated him while he slept. Waking up in a new prison had been quite a shock. He was still struggling with it.

Later, all along death row, cells buzzed open as those who had the luxury of showers returned to their cells. Popcorn was the last. He shot Remo the V-for-victory sign as he passed the cell. But the gesture was made ironic by the hunted look deep in his dark eyes.

After the guards were gone, Popcorn asked, "What's the good word, my man?"

"Saw my lawyer," Remo said in a remote voice.

"I hope you got better news than I did."

"He told me I have an excellent chance of getting fried in the next five years."

"Five!" Popcorn guffawed. "Hell, man, he was jivin' you! You're next after me."

Remo stopped pacing like a man who had been impaled by an icy thought. He drifted up to the cinder-block wall that separated him from Popcorn's cell. Cell Number 1.

"Bullshit," Remo said hotly. But his voice was anxious.

"Man, you know I'm next. That's why they got me in the cell next door from ol' Sparky. You got the next cell up. What that tell you?"

"I can't be ahead of everyone else on the row," Remo said. "I just got here."

"Oh, yes, you can," Popcorn returned. "You done killed a hack. None of them others got that distinc-

tion in their jacket. Truth to tell, my man, you got
Ted Bundy's old cell. Now, you think about that a
spell."

Remo sat on his cot heavily. The color drained
from his face like water down a porcelain sink.

After a while he asked a dull-voiced question.
"Who's Ted Bundy?"

"Shee-it!" Popcorn said in disgust. "Where you
been livin'? In a cave?"

7

That night, beef and rice were served for dinner.
The beef was gray and Remo decided to pass it up.
Although he wanted to keep up his strength, he had
no taste for meat. He wondered if it was because of
the bad news he had received.

But he ate all the rice and wanted more. He found
a single grain clinging to the side of his plastic tray
and he greedily took it in his mouth, holding it
there, tasting its pristine starchy purity, until slowly,
reluctantly, he chewed it to a liquid and swallowed
the taste.

"How often do they serve rice here?" Remo called
out.

"Two, three times a week," Popcorn told him.
"Wish it was more. They screw up the pasta, can't
cook decent potatoes no matter how they do 'em up,
but rice is something even a state cook can't screw
up."

"Amen," Remo said. He started feeling better; his

head even felt clearer. A calmness overtook him and he wondered if it was the grotesque pink coloration of the walls finally getting to him.

Before lights-out, the C.O. who did the head count stopped at Remo's cell and wondered, "I know you from somewhere?"

Remo didn't recognize the man and shrugged.

The guard pressed on. "You look familiar. Something about the eyes. Ever been busted in Coral Gables?"

"I've never been to Coral Gables. I'm from Newark."

"Never been north of Delaware myself," the guard said in a puzzled voice.

"Maybe you be lovers in a past life," Popcorn put in loudly.

He was ignored. The guard inched closer to the bars.

"I'm going to place you, Dead Man," he said. His voice was neither threatening nor insulting. He used the term from long habit. "I don't suppose you've ever been on television."

"No," Remo said, ending the conversation.

The guard went away, the progress of his leaving marked by receding door clangings.

"What was that all about?" Popcorn demanded after the lights were out.

"Search me," Remo said as he stripped for bed.

Sleep took him slowly. He had just started to drift off when he saw a face. It was not really a face so much as the impression of a face. It was gray. Or the background was gray. All Remo could clearly see was crisp white hair and a pair of rimless eyeglasses. There were no features under the hair and the eyes behind the glasses. Just the outline of an angular face. Drowsily Remo tried to peer closer. Just as the features started to resolve themselves, he snapped awake.

Lying awake, Remo fought to hold that fading

image, as if, even awake, he could summon up that amorphous face in his mind's eye and force its true features to come into focus.

But like a lamp burn on the retina, it remained blurry until it faded. Finally Remo slept. He dreamed of rice. Huge mountains of steamed rice. It made his mouth water, even in sleep.

8

"I been dwellin' on it," Popcorn was saying in between mouthfuls of the same scrambled eggs that Remo was dumping into the open toilet bowl rather than smell them a second longer. "And I decided I'm one lucky dude."

"How do you figure that?" Remo asked, wondering if he should try the hash browns. He brought a plastic forkful to his lips, touched it with his tongue, and decided to pass. The toilet flushed a second time.

"This could be Red China and not America."

"Uh-huh."

"In China," Popcorn continued solemnly, "they give you a bullet to the back of the brain soon as they find you guilty. Then they send your folks a bill for the bullet. You know what a bullet costs in Red China? Thirteen cents. Hell, the bullet I used on Condoleeza couldn't have set me back more than a nickel. But that's communism for you. Even bullets cost more."

"I thought you said you cut her."

"I did. I cut her, then I shot her. I was honked off, okay?"

Remo stared into his orange juice. This time, there were no little flecks of pulp, which told him it was probably diluted from concentrate. He decided it was better than nothing and started to sip it slowly, hoping it wouldn't burn his tongue and throat.

Popcorn's voice rose. "In France, they used to use a guillotine. It supposed to be quick, but I read once of a dude who had his head taken off for real, who died so quick and slick his brain didn't know it. *Chuck* went that guillotine. *Sluck* went his ol' head. *Plop* it go, into the basket. And there it lay, blinking and trying to talk through the blood that come up from his poor mouth. Except the poor sucker ain't got no windpipe to blow his words out with."

Halfway through the orange juice, Remo wondered how many times he'd have to flush the toilet before the water was fit to drink. He decided, reluctantly, that the answer was a disappointing never.

"Hanging's worse, though," Popcorn went on in a merry voice. "You hang, and not only do you strangle to death, but your neck done break and you get a headache and a hard-on at the same time. You probably piss your pants to boot. Nobody should die hanging, not even a Puerto Rican."

By that remark, Remo took it to mean that as in New Jersey, Puerto Rican inmates were considered the lowest rung of the prison social ladder. He could never figure out why that was. He had known an Eskimo up in Trenton who was doing a dime for manslaughter. A minority of one, but everyone liked him.

"I am not a fan of gassin', either," Popcorn was saying. His chipper tone of voice rose in inverse proportion to the cheerfulness of his topic. "They strap you down in a little room and the cowards pull a lever in another room, droppin' these cyanide crystals into a bedpan of acid. Least, I heard it said it was a bedpan. That's where you get your gas. Imagine sitting there with those clouds billowing up around your hangdog face, knowin' that even if you held your breath, you were only prolongin' the agony."

"I hear you go quick that way," Remo said.

"Yeah?" Popcorn said testily. "Well, I hear your eyes bug out of your head, you go all purply in the face and drool like fuckin' Howdy Doody. No way I wanna go out drooling. I had my dignity in life. I wanna go the same way, with a little style, Jim. A touch of class. The chair ain't so bad when you think about it. You get to sit down and you kinda go out on your own throne." He allowed himself a dry chuckle.

"I take it you changed your mind about throwing yourself at Crusher McGurk," Remo said airily.

"What, and cut my days short? No chance, Jim."

Down the corridor, the electronic doors began to buzz and roll, presaging approaching guards.

"Damn!" Popcorn said. "He be early for these trays. I been talkin' when I shoulda been eatin'. You know, this ol' prison food never tasted as good to me as it does now."

The door sounds grew closer. Two pairs of footsteps became audible through the remaining door. Voices along the row, mostly men talking to themselves, suddenly hushed.

"I don't think they're here for the trays," Remo said.

"I think you be right, Jim."

Remo drifted up to the bars of his cell. Maybe it was news of his appeal.

Officiously a guard swept past his cell. Accompanying him was a heavyset sixtyish man in a civilian work uniform. The man moved furtively, his hand up to his face to shield it, as if he were a convicted felon. He was not manacled.

The two men swept out of view.

"No, man," Popcorn protested. "It's too soon. I don't go till Tuesday. Tuesday, you hear!" His voice jumped to an excitable high C.

"Pipe down," the guard growled. "We'll get around to you."

The sound of a wheel turning told Remo that the iron door to the electric-chair room had been opened. It was closed by a huge wheel like on a submarine hatch. There was a medieval sound to the door swinging on seldom-used hinges.

"Just tap on the glass when you're done, Haines," the guard said. "I'll be right here."

The door squealed shut.

"How you doing, Popcorn?" the guard asked in good humor.

"I was fuckin' chipper until a minute ago, hack," Popcorn said uneasily. "I was the chipperest Dead Man you ever saw. Now I don't know."

"You'll feel plenty hot, homeboy, once they got your throne all wired up." The guard's laugh was derisive, full-throated.

"I was just thinking that the chair ain't a bad way to go," Popcorn muttered. "Now I ain't so sure."

"Oh, it's not bad. Lethal injection is better, though." The guard's voice was matter-of-fact, just slightly tinged with cheerfulness.

"You don't say," Popcorn's voice was saying as Remo settled back on his cot.

"Yeah, once they cannulate the vein, the worst is over."

"What's 'cannulate'?"

"It means they plug in an intravenous line. It's fascinating to watch how they do it. They plug you in and the execution technician stands on the other side of a wall. First he pumps in something to knock you out. Then they squirt in the curare to paralyze your muscles. And then comes the show-stopper, potassium chloride to arrest your heart action."

"Doesn't sound all that quick to me," Popcorn said doubtfully.

"It's quicker than Sparky. Sometimes—"

"Don't tell me no more!" Popcorn said quickly. "I know all about Sparky. They zap you and you breathe your last right then and there. If you lucky."

"They never go that quick," the guard said informatively. "Remember that big black buck, Shango?"

"Now, don't you be callin' Shango no buck!" Popcorn snapped. "He was a righteous dude."

"Remember when the lights flickered the morning he went?"

"Yeah."

"Remember how many times?"

"No! Stop talkin' at me! I can't think no more!"

"Four times, Popcorn, Count 'em. Four. The first time the leather strap holding the electrode to his leg burned clean away. They had to shut off the juice to fix it. And Shango sat there all strapped in for his last ride, his head lolling off to one side, and there was smoke coming out of his ears."

"No way! No way, man! Shango went out wearin' a hood. No way you could tell if his ears be smokin'. You lyin' to me, motherfuck, you tryin' to rattle me."

"Now that you mention it," the guard admitted, "the smoke was coming up out from under the hood. We only found out after they took the hood off that it was coming out of his ears. The executioner said it was the first time he'd ever seen it. Usually smoke comes out of the mouth or up from the shirt collar. I guess the chest hairs burn or something. But you don't have to worry about that, boy. You're too young to have much chest hair."

Popcorn said nothing.

The guard went on. "Anyway, where was I? Oh, right. They jolted him again once they replaced the strap, but the doc found a heartbeat. So they had to hit him four times."

"Did he move?" Popcorn asked in a pathetic voice. "Did he say anything while this was happenin' to him?"

"He couldn't. The electricity, it freezes the muscles. Paralyzes your lungs too. You sit there, can't move, can't breathe, smelling the smoke of your own burning hair while your brains cook like eggs."

Suddenly the unmistakable sound of violent vomiting came from Popcorn's cell. And suddenly Remo smelled the breakfast eggs he had flushed down the toilet.

"Did you have to do that?" Remo demanded in a loud voice.

The guard suddenly appeared in front of Remo's cell. He was grinning broadly.

"My mistake," he said. "I forgot they serve eggs on Mondays. Well, one good thing came out of it. When your turn comes, Williams, I won't have to waste my breath repeating all the grisly details to you."

Remo grabbed the cell-door bars tightly. "Why, you—"

"Temper, temper," the guard cautioned. "Oops, I think I hear the executioner man tapping on the Door of Doom."

The guard went away and opened the squealing door.

"All done?" he asked, suddenly serious-voiced. "Good. Come on, then. Let's get you out of here."

The two men went past Remo's cell quickly, but not so quickly that Remo didn't catch a glimpse of the executioner's face. The sight triggered a cold shock in the pit of his stomach. There was something familiar about that furtive, weathered face. But the man passed from view before Remo could see it clearly.

"Sorry I had to take you in through the row," the guard was telling the other man, "but I figured it would be quicker."

The other said nothing in reply, and the first door control buzzed open.

The guard's voice rang back. "I'll send someone back with a mop," he promised. "Unless you want to consider it a second helping."

The guard's laughter was swallowed by the closing doors and a renewed spitting coming from Popcorn's cell.

"If he comes back," Remo said, "I'd throw it in his face. What have you got to lose?"

"He won't come back," Popcorn said miserably. "He know better than that."

"Probably."

"Hey, Remo?"

"Yeah?" Remo said, noticing the unexpected use of his first name.

"Remember what I said about the yard?"

"Yeah."

"Well, it back on. I'll take Crusher over having my brains sizzled any day."

"We go to the yard today, you know."

"Today?" Popcorn croaked.

"Today."

"Shit. I forgot it was today. Shit. I done ate my last meal, then."

"I wouldn't go up against Crusher if I were you."

"My life ain't worth the squirt that brought me into the world, man. I want my death to amount to something. You my only friend in the joint, Remo. Shee-it."

"What?"

"I just realized I threw up for the last time. And now I'm gonna take me a last piss." The zipper sound came next.

"Why don't you save it?" Remo suggested.

"For what?"

"For Crusher."

"Good thinkin'. Uh-oh, here come the man with the mop."

A guard pushed a steel-wheeled cart with one hand and carried the mop in his other. He had trouble managing both tasks simultaneously. The mop slipped from his held-high grasp and he cursed and let the yarn head fall. He was dragging it after him as he passed Remo's field of vision.

Popcorn's cell grated open and the guard said, "I'll trade you. A new mop for an old tray."

"Deal, sucker," said Popcorn.

"Hurry it up. I gotta wait for the mop."

"Be just a second." The mop made sloppy sounds in the adjoining cell.

Remo, contemplating the ceiling, was suddenly aware of the guard staring at him through the bars of his cell.

"The night shift has been talking about you, Williams."

"Good for them." Out of the corner of his eye Remo noticed the guard clutched a folded newspaper in his hand. His eyes kept going back to the paper. It was a tabloid.

"Ever been in Yuma, Williams?" he asked.

"No."

"How about Detroit?"

"Never."

"Then you got a twin who should be on the Letterman show or something."

"I'm an orphan."

"They call him Dead Man too," the guard said.

"Who?" Remo forced his voice to be bored. But curiosity was creeping into it.

"Your twin. The one they call the Dead Man."

"We're all Dead Men on this block," Remo said. He shifted position so that he could see the folded-down top of the newspaper. The upside down headline seemed to say: STARTLING NEW EVIDENCE. SAME ASSASSIN KILLED ROY ORBISON, LUCILLE BALL, AND AYATOLLAH KHOMEINI!"

Remo didn't have to look any closer. The guard obviously had hold of a copy of the *National Enquirer*. Remo instantly lost interest. Only morons read the *Enquirer*.

"Well, this Dead Man makes Schwarzenegger look like Rick Moranis," the guard was saying as he opened the paper. "Says here he was sighted in Arizona breaking tanks with his bare hands during the Japanese occupation."

"Can't be me," Remo said. "I was born after World War II."

"The Japanese occupation of Yuma, Arizona. Last Christmas."

"If you believe the Japanese invaded Arizona," Remo grunted, "then I guess you can believe a man can break a tank with his bare hands." He sighed. Sometimes the guards had it worse than the prisoners. Most prisoners got out, one way or the other. But most guards were lifers in their way. It often took a toll. Some went mean. Others got simple. This guard was obviously one of the simple ones.

"They must have buried you pretty deep in Jersey for you not to know about the Japanese thing last Christmas."

"Never heard of it," Remo said.

Popcorn's voice broke in. "I'm done," he said.

The guard retrieved the mop and then came to Remo's cell for his tray.

"Mind leaving that paper?" Remo asked casually, his eyes on the paper wadded under the guard's arm.

"You know the rule. Dead Men aren't allowed to read in their cells."

"We're not allowed in the prison library either."

"I don't make the rules." And the guard went on down the line, collecting trays.

When the din began to settle down, Popcorn called out, "Why were you jivin' him, man?"

"I wasn't jiving him."

"You serious? You mean you didn't hear about the Jap thing last Christmas?"

"We beat the Japanese nearly fifty years ago."

"Maybe so. But a few of them snuck back and spit in Uncle Sam's face. Wonder what that Dead Man thing was he was runnin' off at the mouth about?"

"Search me," Remo said. Disinterest crept back into his voice like a sluggish tide onto a mud flat. He wondered if the guard had been trying to make a duck of him and if Popcorn hadn't joined in just to amuse himself.

The ten-o'clock head count same swiftly, and after that lunch, which consisted of leftover beef and rice from the previous day. Remo flushed the beef away and attacked the rice with eagerness. Compared to the night before, it tasted mushy, but it was rice. He ate ravenously, surprised at how much he enjoyed the rice. He never used to like rice all that much.

At three o'clock the call came.

"Head count. Line up for the yard!"

Remo felt his blood run cold.

"Showtime!" Popcorn said jauntily.

"You're not going through with it?" Remo hissed.

"Don't know. Maybe I'll fight. Maybe I'll hit the fence. But we'll both find out."

The cell doors all along death row buzzed open and the men stepped out in their apricot T-shirts and formed short lines between the sealed section-control doors. Then, all at once, these doors opened and they began to march through Grand Central and out into the yard.

Once out into the sun, Popcorn started for the fence. Remo grabbed him by the back of his T-shirt.

"Where are you going?"

"I said maybe I'll hit the fence. Maybe I will."

Remo spun the little con around. "Don't be a fool. Even if you make the first fence, the hacks'll nail you before you get to the second one."

Popcorn's eyes were bleak and flat as unpolished onyx.

"A lead pill's bitter medicine, my man. But Florida juice is pure poison."

Popcorn turned to pull away, but Remo only tightened his grip.

"Oh, almost forgot," Popcorn said. He extracted a mashed pack of Camels from his dungaree pocket. A matchbook was wedged into the cellophane wrapper. He slapped it into Remo's open hand.

"No time for a last smoke," he said with a wide, devil-may-care grin. "Don't want to cut my breath for runnin'."

Those were the last words that Mohammed "Popcorn" Diladay ever spoke, because so suddenly that Remo received only a momentary sense of an approaching shadow, Crusher McGurk suddenly loomed up behind Popcorn. He towered over the little con like a human mountain.

Popcorn's eyes read the look on Remo's face and started to lift to the sky. His mouth opened to speak. He never got the words out.

For Crusher McGurk gathered Popcorn up bodily and turned him around. He brought his blubbery mouth to Popcorn's own surprised lips and attacked it like a human leech.

Popocorn's feet started kicking. His fists flailed. Remo moved fast. But not fast enough, because with a horrible animal cry, McGurk suddenly reared back, his mouth bloody. He dropped Popcorn to the shimmering asphalt and threw his head back, howling.

Remo froze, thinking that McGurk had gotten the worst of it. Then he saw Popcorn, quivering on the ground, trying to hold the squirting blood in his mouth with both hands.

And Crusher McGurk, his head thrown back triumphantly, made a show of swallowing what was in his mouth.

"You son of a bitch!" Remo blazed. He lunged for the

burly con. McGurk lifted one massive paw and tried to swat Remo away. Remo ducked under the blow. He was conscious of the other inmates closing in, trying to keep the fight from the guards as long as possible.

"Take his head off, McGurk!" one hissed vehemently.

McGurk's other hand swept around. Remo's forearm, all lean muscle and bone, shot up to intercept it. McGurk's fist struck and bounced off. McGurk howled and grabbed his injured hand. He froze, looking at his bone-shocked arm with stupefied eyes. Their focus passed his hand and locked on Remo.

"I'm gonna have more than your tongue, cop," he roared. Too loudly, as it turned out.

"Riot in the yard!" a guard howled.

Remo knew he'd have only a minute at most. He kicked McGurk in his huge beer belly. McGurk doubled over and Remo broke his front teeth with his fist. McGurk spit out more blood. This time it was his own. He went down on one knee as the guards started shoving and clubbing at the outer circle of inmates. Remo knew he would have to finish McGurk here and now if he wanted to live to see the electric chair.

Then a strange thing happened. Like sharks sensing blood, the other inmates turned on McGurk. He was kicked on all sides and rabbit-punched in the face.

Shock must have paralyzed the big convict, because he simply crouched there like a deformed idol as blow after blow rained down on him. But stubbornly, he wouldn't fall. Remo came around to the side and, without thinking, chopped at the back of his thick neck with the side of his open hand. The first blow sounded meaty; the second made a crunching noise.

Remo stepped back. Crusher's eyes rolled up in his head. His mouth went slack, but amazingly, he held his position, as if his body was unable to comprehend the damage done to it.

Then a convict came out of the packed crowd carrying a weighted sock. And while two others held McGurk, he laid blow after blow on McGurk's dumbfounded face.

In the time it took for Remo to step back two paces, Crusher McGurk's face had become a mask of chewed meat. But that didn't stop his attacker, a black man with only four fingers on his left hand. He continued to wield the weighted sock until it was torn apart, spilling its contents—broken razor blades and old C batteries.

McGurk went down on his ruin of a face, and the black con, hearing the guards' approach, hastily tossed the ruined sock on Popcorn's heaving stomach, saying, "That's for takin' my finger off, dickhead."

The crowd dispersed, giving the guards room to move in.

Remo hung back. Popcorn lay on his back, his eyes wide and catching the bright sunlight like black jewels, blood oozing up between his dark fingers. Remo knelt beside him.

"Just hold on, okay?" he urged.

Little red bubbles broke over Popcorn's fingers, and Remo had to turn away.

The guards swarmed over them then. Remo was rudely pulled off and shoved to one side.

"What happened here?" the captain of the guards demanded.

Before Remo could respond, one of the inmates called out, "McGurk jumped Popcorn. Bit his tongue off, just like he did last year. Only Popcorn had a weapon. He paid McGurk back."

"Yeah, that right," another voice added. "McGurk picked the wrong fish this time. Serve the cocksucker right." This from the black con who had attacked McGurk with the deadly sock.

There were no dissenting accounts of the incident and the guards quickly began herding the inmates back toward the compound. The inmates hesitated. More than a few wanted to know how Popcorn was. No one asked after McGurk.

The guards on the tower catwalks fired shots into the air to get them moving, immediately training their weapons into the crowd once they had the yard's attention.

Hastily the inmates formed three lines and filed into the main building. A voice behind Remo whispered in his ear, "You done us all a good turn, taking on McGurk. And we appreciate it."

When his cell door clanged shut on Remo, he felt emptier than at any time since he'd found himself in Florida State Prison.

The prison remained under lockdown into lights-out. Supper was not served, and Remo wondered if Popcorn had finally cheated the chair.

He hoped for Popcorn's sake it was true.

9

In his dreams, Remo was a free man.

Except for the old Oriental.

He was scaling a sheer wall. The old Oriental looked down from the thirtieth floor of the building to the twenty-eighth floor, where Remo clung to the tinted glass facade like a human spider.

"You must move faster," the old Oriental squeaked. "I am twice your age and you lag like an old woman on a hot day." His face was a map of wrinkles, like papier-mâché drying in the sun. His eyes were as

clear as agates, and as hard. They looked at Remo
with contempt.

"I'm climbing as fast as I can," Remo returned.
The sharpness of the old Oriental's gaze hurt him in
an indefinable way.

The old Oriental's mouth thinned disapprovingly
over the strands of straggly beard that fluttered from
his chin.

"That is your mistake," he snapped. "I am not
teaching you to climb this edifice, but to use its
inner strength to lift you to your goal. Arms that
climb, tire. Buildings do not tire. Therefore you will
use the building's strength, not your own."

Remo wanted to say that was bullshit, but he had
already gotten this far by following instructions. His
feet were splayed outward on the quarter-inch molding around the big sandwich-glass window. His palms
pressed the glass, fingers flat, not clutching, but
allowing the surface tension of his skin against the
smooth glass to hold him in place. He felt like a bug.

And above him the old Oriental resumed his as-
cent like a monkey in a jet-black silk robe. Even the
bottoms of his sandals were black as old tires.

Remo raised his hands over his head. He took hold
of the molding above the window with bone-hard
fingertips. He pulled downward. And like a gargantuan window shade, the facade seemed to drop under him. Except that the building stayed on its
foundation. It was Remo who went up, as effortlessly
as if climbing a helpful glass ladder.

Floor by floor, he followed the old Oriental until
they were together on the rooftop. The old Oriental
led him to a trapdoor and they slipped down into a
dim hallway.

"Do as I do," the old Oriental whispered.

Remo followed him as soundlessly as a drifting
wind. The old Oriental moved toward a black metal

door in which a red pinpoint light glowed where the keyhole should have been.

"If we break it, it'll trigger an alarm," Remo warned.

"Then I will not break it," the old Oriental said. "Observe, now."

The old man placed his fingertips over the red pinpoint and drummed them silently until the light turned green. He pushed the door open casually and Remo followed him, a wondering expression on his face.

"How'd you do that? It's supposed to be impossible without a magnetic passcard."

"It is electrical," the old man said.

"Yeah?"

"So. I am electrical too. But my electricity is stronger."

"That doesn't make any sense," Remo told the old Oriental as they moved down the corridor, two shadows in a deeper blackness. Then: "When are you going to teach me to do that?"

"When I sense your natural energies are equal to the task."

"What's that in real time?"

"Never."

And Remo felt stung to his core.

They turned a corner and almost walked into a brown-uniformed security guard who stood before an unmarked door with an assault rifle raised protectively before him.

Remo hung back. Seeing the old Oriental continue his floating stride unchecked, he followed after him. The guard was looking right at them, evidently not registering their presence.

Then the guard looked away, and the old man froze. Remo froze too. And when the guard's gaze stared in their direction once more, he moved on, crossing the hallway with Remo close behind him, like his shadow.

Safely in another hallway, Remo wanted to know how it had been done.

"A man, when he looks directly at something, will perceive only something out of the ordinary," he was told. "You and I were part of the movement of air through this dark place, and therefore part of the vibration. But the corners of the eye will register any movement. That is why we stopped when we did."

They came to another pinpoint red light.

"Let me try this one," Remo offered. He placed his fingertips against the plate and started tapping in a dissynchronous rhythm.

The light remained red.

Impatiently the old Oriental stepped in and tapped the plate once. The light turned green.

"Was that you or me?" Remo asked as they closed the door behind them.

"It is all in the nails," the old Oriental said, shaking his wide sleeves free of his thin wrists. His nails were like pale blades. "Come, we are almost to our objective."

They entered a room filled with a low-level humming. As Remo's eyes adjusted to the darkness, he saw the jerky movement of computer tape reels behind plastic panels. An air conditioner expelled chilled chemically tainted air.

"Which one do you think is our friend?" Remo breathed.

"It does not matter. We will destroy them all."

Suddenly a pair of panels glowed in dull green light. They looked like flat blank eyes.

And a warm, generous, but completely unhuman voice spoke. "Welcome. And good-bye."

Then the center of the floor split down the middle and separated into identical falling panels.

Remo leapt for the only safety within reach. A hanging fluorescent light. He felt a sudden sharp weight on his right ankle and looked down.

Looking back up at him was the old Oriental's seamed countenance. He had Remo's ankle in one birdlike claw. But far more arresting was what was visible beyond the Oriental's robed form.

It looked like a gargantuan electronic well. It pulsed with a million lights and seemed to go down beyond the foundation of the building and into the bedrock itself.

The two halves of the floor lay flat against the north and south walls of the square well.

"We goofed, Little Father," Remo said. "The main computer isn't in this room. The whole building's a giant mainframe."

"Do you have a firm grip?" the old Oriental demanded in a squeaky voice. He was staring down into the pulsing lights of the abyss. A cold draft came up to flutter his hemline.

"I do," Remo said, looking up at the cracks forming in the ceiling around the light fixture. "But this fixture doesn't."

The old Oriental looked up with wistful features.

"It is not strong enough to support us both," he said sadly.

"I guess this is the end."

"For me. Not for you. You are the future, but I am the past. Farewell, my son."

And the old Oriental simply let go. As Remo watched in horror, the old man tumbled past banks of lights, his face set, almost serene in its fatalism.

"Chiun! No!" Remo screamed. And woke up.

Remo rolled out of bed. He was soaking in cold sweat. His fingers clutched his pillow in a death grip. He tried letting go, but they were like claws. He took a deep breath and started to feel his fingers warm with blood. Feeling returned to them, and slowly, painfully, the pillow dropped to the cold floor.

In the darkness, Remo whispered a single name: "Chiun. . . ."

10

The Master of Sinanju took the shore road that led to the rock formation inscribed in the scrolls of his ancestors as the Horns of Welcome, which framed the normally forbidding waters of the West Korea Bay.

Here the shore was sand for a stretch. On either side, the sand gave way to grim granite rocks, covered with barnacles, that jutted out to the pounding surf like broken, petrified fingers. The sun was setting into the water, turning the gray choppiness of the sea the dull crimson of coagulating blood.

It lacked exactly thirty minutes to sunset. The appointed hour. And as Chiun, Reigning Master of Sinanju, stepped onto the sand, out beyond the rocks a submarine emblazoned with the flag of the barbarian nation called, variously, America, the United States, and the USA, broke the water with such violence that it seemed as if the sea were hemorrhaging.

The name on the bow was *Harlequin*. A hatch clanged and a seaman in white clambered up. He brought a device set with twin disks of ground glass to his eyes so that his weak white vision could discern the minimal distance from his vessel to the shore of Sinanju, pearl of Asia, birthplace of the sun source, and the home of Chiun, in the northern reaches of divided Korea.

Chiun placed a hand to his forehead. It was a sign to the weak-eyed white that he was not yet ready to leave his home village. The seaman lowered his glasses and, like a fool, unnecessarily waved in response. Then he disappeared into his craft. Finally the vessel submerged, to sleep in the cold waters of the West Korea Bay another night, until the Master of Sinanju placed his hand over his heart to signal that he was ready to return to his adopted land.

Chiun was not ready to return to the United States. He spun about, his purple robes pressing against his spindly arms and legs in the persistent sea breeze. Even though the wind was coming off the water, still the nostrils of the Master of Sinanju picked up the scent of boiling rice from the cooking pots of his village. And mixed with that, the unpleasant stink of burning pork and beef.

As the village square came into view, Chiun saw the women bent over their pots. They scarcely looked up at him, who had returned to Sinanju after a long absence, bearing new treasure for the glory of the village. So much treasure this year that there was no room for it in the wooden house on the hill called the House of the Masters and Chiun had had the strong men of the village put it in the spare treasure house, which was of rude stone and decorated with sea shells.

Yet, despite this abundance of riches, the men who were sweeping the square clear of the day's dust paid him little heed.

The Master of Sinanju comforted himself with the thought that they were busy. It was no slight when his industrious villagers went about their tasks with such fervor that they did not pause to engage him in conversation or to thank him for the glory he brought to the village.

The Master of Sinanju looked around his village. Where other eyes might see mud huts or fishing shacks, he saw tradition. Where foreign eyes might see an outwardly poor village, he saw a center of culture that had stood on this spot for five thousand years, inhabited by a bloodline that had been unbroken for almost as long. It was rare when an outsider was allowed to marry into the village of Sinanju, rarer still when one of the village dwelt in the outside world for long periods of time as he had.

The clear eyes of the Master of Sinanju drank in the sight of his ancestral village with pride. Only by his labors, his sacrifice, did the people continue to eat, despite the poor fishing and the exhausted farm soil. Only by his upholding of ancient traditions did Sinanju live more secure than any village, nay, any city in North Korea. It was safer even than Pyongyang, the communist capital.

The Master of Sinanju's searching gaze alighted on a circle of children playing in the shadow of the Gong of Judgment. A happy smile wreathed his wrinkled countenance.

The children of the village. For as long as Chiun lived, none of them would ever be sent home to the sea—drowned in the bay for lack of food to nourish them. The adults might take that for granted, but the children would not.

Chiun glided toward the children, his eyes twinkling with wisdom to be shared.

"Ho, children of my village," cried the Master of Sinanju in the low, quaking voice he used to recite tales of the House of Sinanju, the most feared assassins in history. "Gather around me, for I have come to tell you stories of the barbarian West."

The children converged on him like pigeons after corn.

"More stories!" a butterball boy squealed.

"Come," Chiun said, shooing them away so he could settle onto a flat stone. The children sat, folded their legs, and placed their tiny hands on their knees. They looked up at him with wide innocent eyes.

"Tonight," Chiun began, "while the sun is still to

be seen and our bellies await the evening meal, I will tell you the story of how the white men sailed to the moon."

A little girl stuck out her tongue. "It is not true. How could a white man sail to the moon? It is not in the ocean, except at day, and then it is under the ocean."

"I have told you of the hollow birds that the whites use to go places in their faraway land," Chiun said, raising long-nailed finger.

"Yes!" the children of Sinanju chorused.

"This is a story like that. Let me begin." Chiun deepened his storytelling voice further.

"Now, the days of which I speak were long ago," Chiun said. He touched a girl's button nose. "Before any of you gathered around me were born. In those days I dwelt in this village, and the times were lean. In those days the babies of Sinanju were those who, through my forbearance, were allowed to grow up to become your mothers and fathers, instead of being drowned, for in those days there was no work for the village and the money was almost gone."

"What about the treasure?" the little girl asked.

"The treasure is not for spending," Chiun retorted. "It is the heritage of the village."

"My mother says we would have fuller bellies if the treasure were spent and not hoarded."

"Who is your mother?" Chiun snapped, his cheeks blowing out in sudden fury.

"Poo."

"Ah, I remember Poo," said the Master of Sinanju, gaining control of himself. He would see to that common scold, Poo, later. He went on with his story in a calmer voice.

"I have already told you about the day the white man with a hook for a hand came to this village in his iron boat that sailed under the seas. This man brought to me an offer of much riches if I would journey to his far-off land to train a person of his choosing in the art of Sinanju. Although it was a burden on my frail shoulders . . ." Chiun paused to see if appreciation lighted the faces of the children. When he recognized wonderment, he decided it was good enough and went on.

"Although it was a burden, I accepted this task and journeyed in the cold belly of the ocean to do what was asked of me, for I knew that my trials would feed the babies who are now your parents, and although I knew that some of them would never achieve wisdom enough to appreciate that sacrifice, I nevertheless went on, for I knew even then that those children would one day bear children of their own. And no ordinary children either, but those who understood sacrifice and appreciate the gifts bestowed on them. You children."

The children put their childish hands to their mouths and giggled. Chiun took that as appreciation. He would have preferred respectful silence, however. Bowing of heads would not have been amiss either.

"Now, the days of which I am about to speak are the earliest days of my time in the barbarian land of America. It was the three hundred and thirty-fourth day of the Year of the Dragon, which was, according to the complicated dating used by westerners, the third Tuesday of that second month, on the festival known as Dairy Goat Appreciation Day, during National Secretary's Week, in the year that numbered only 1972, for this land is in truth much younger than Korea.

"On this day," Chiun went on, "the land of America was in turmoil, for one of their strange vessels was nearing the moon. Hearing of this, I hurried to the throne room of the secret King of America, Mad Harold. I have told you of Mad Harold before. And presenting myself to this man, I said to him, 'I have heard tales from the remote provinces of your land that some of your subjects were nearing the moon.' And Mad Harold replied that this was so. He was exceedingly calm about this news, although I could detect a trace of pride in his tones.

"Now, when I heard this news, I too grew excited. No man had been to the moon in thousands of years, since Master Shang had walked so far north that his feet actually trod upon the cold wastes of the moon. And I shared this with Mad Harold, who seemed not surprised to learn that Koreans had journeyed to the moon before whites. And Mad Harold told me that other whites had been to the moon before that time. I was suspicious of this, and questioned Mad Harold about this closely, and he told me that the first whites to land on the moon did so in their year of 1969. To which I replied that Master Shang achieved the moon in our Year of the Heron. So, remember, we were the first. And do not forget that Shang walked.

"Now, knowing that the moon the Master Shang had visited was all ice and snow inhabited by white snow bears, I asked Mad Harold, King of America, if they had found rich cities on the moon to conquer, and he said no. I asked him if they had discovered mines of silver and gold, I asked him if there were slaves there, and he said no and he said no. I asked him if the meat of the white snow bears was the object of these expeditions, which I was told in confidence cost the ransom of a Japanese prince, and he said no."

By this point, the children sat round-mouthed.

"These words of Mad Harold puzzled me greatly, for I could see no reason for these expeditions and I asked him what his brave sailors brought back from these perilous journeys that replenished the treasury the cost of undertaking them. And his answer was so strange that I immediately returned to my scrolls

and entered what he told me in the histories of
Sinanju.

"And do you know what these whites, these spend-
thrifts, brought back from the moon after their fright-
ful journeys of many days?" Chiun asked.

"What, O Master?" the children of Sinanju chorused.

"Rocks," breathed the Master of Sinanju. "Common stones. I myself was allowed to hold one of
these in my very hands. They were neither beautiful
nor valuable. And seeing this, I returned to the
castle of Mad King Harold and I said to him, 'I have
seen with my wise old eyes the stones your moon
expeditions have brought back on their arduous journeys and I am prepared to bring to you as many
similar stones as you desire for half the money you
squander on these moon voyages.'" Chiun paused
dramatically. "And do you know what Mad King
Harold said to me?"

"What?" a dirty-haired boy piped up.

"He declined my generous and intelligent offer,
saying that only stones from the moon would do,"
Chiun said disdainfully.

At that, the children of Sinanju burst into giggling.

"Have you ever been to the moon, Master Chiun?"
the little girl who was the daughter of Poo asked.

"No," Chiun replied, "for soon after this, the whites
stopped sending their sailors to the moon, which
shows that even whites can learn if they repeat a
stupid thing often enough."

The children smiled. Everyone knew that whites
were dense. Why else did the Supreme Creator give
them stupid round eyes which to behold the world,
and exile them to live across the sea?

"When are you going back to America?" asked the
daughter of Poo, who Chiun noted was cursed with
her mother's incessant tongue.

"Why do you ask?" Chiun asked.

"Because my mother said that when you return to

the village, you always bring misfortune. And you are stingy with your gold."

"Your mother said that?" Chiun asked quickly. His hazel eyes narrowed. The little girl nodded. She was chubby and in her round face Chiun could see a hint of the fat face of Poo. "Your mother is very free with her tongue," Chiun said quietly.

"She does yell a lot," the little girl said vaguely.

An older boy raised his hand, and Chiun nodded in his direction.

"Will you tell us a story of the white man whom you had exalted to greatness by teaching him the art of Sinanju?"

"I have many tales of Remo," Chiun said proudly. "Let me think of a good one—"

"Where is he now?" another boy interrupted. "Why did you not bring him?"

Chiun hesitated. How could he tell them the shameful truth—that the one white in all the world who had been allowed to learn the art of the sun source now languished in a prison? Chiun bowed his old head. It was too shameful a story to tell to children. He searched his mind for a way to answer the question truthfully without bringing disgrace on his head.

Just then, the dinner gong reverberated over the sleepy village of Sinanju, saving the Master of Sinanju the trouble. He stood up and spanked the dust from his magnificent robes.

"Come," he said. "It is time to fill our bellies. I will tell you a story of Remo another time."

And the Master of Sinanju strode off, leading the children into the communal eating era. As he topped a hill, he saw the corpulent shape of Poo the Tart-tongued, and his face hardened and his gait picked up as he hurried in her direction.

11

Remo lay awake the rest of the night thinking about the old Oriental. The dream had shaken him. There was something almost tangible about the images, particularly the old Oriental. Even hours later, his wizened face hovered clearly in Remo's mind's eye. Every wrinkle, every inflection in his voice. It was as if he had actually known the little man. But as Remo searched his memory, he couldn't recall ever having seen him in real life.

It was strange. In his dream, the little Asian had a name. Chiun. Remo couldn't remember ever having had a dream in which one of the figments of his imagination had a name. Remo even knew how to spell it. There was an I that wasn't pronounced.

It was a pretty sophisticated concept for his subconscious mind, Remo reflected. Why not Chang? He had heard the name Chang before. Many Chinese were named Chang. It was like the name Jones over here. He had never heard of a Chiun, however.

After a while Remo drifted off. The morning buzzer jolted him awake too soon. Slowly Remo got into his dungarees and apricot-colored T-shirt. He hated the T-shirt almost as much as the pink cell walls. He wished it was blue. Or the walls were blue. These pastels reminded him of a cheap department-store print.

Before breakfast was shoved through the slot, word

raced down the row that Crusher McGurk had died during the night.

"What about Popcorn?" Remo asked urgently.

A voice replied with a gruff, "Don't no one know, man. But that boy, he got spunk. That how he got his name."

"How did he get his name?" Remo asked suddenly.

"When the little dude came down the line first time, he was jokin' and jivin', tellin' the hacks that when his time come to set his ass on Sparky, he was bringing a thing of Jiffy Pop with him. Said it was for the row. After that, he was Popcorn."

Remo grunted. He wondered if Popcorn, wherever he was, had any of that spirit left in him.

Remo told the guard, "Thanks, but no thanks," when he appeared with the tray. It was ham and beans. The C.O. shrugged and started away, but Remo called after him, "Hey, what's the word on Popcorn?"

"Does it matter? He's scheduled to go tomorrow."

"Yeah, hack," Remo growled. "It matters to me." He fell back into his bunk and suddenly remembered the pack of Camels in his dungaree pockets. He fished them out and lit one up.

The first puff sent him coughing. The second was a little less harsh. His lungs only burned like sulfur. Remo managed to smoke half of it before his head started aching. He snuffed the butt against the floor and carefully replaced the remaining half in the pack after the tip had cooled. No telling how long the pack would have to last him.

It was late afternoon when two guards escorted Popcorn to his cell. The little con walked in chains, with his head bowed low.

Remo waited until the guards were gone before he hissed out a greeting. "How's it going, kid?"

The sound that came back was mewing. Remo couldn't make it out. Somewhere down the line, a taunting voice said, "Hey, Popcorn, what's the matter? Pussycat got your tongue?"

And from Popcorn's cell came a protracted whimpering that turned Remo's blood cold. It went on for an hour. A picture of Popcorn, his face buried in his pillow, unable to speak, leapt into Remo's head.

Remo pulled out the half-cigarette and a single match, then pushed the pack out into the corridor.

"Here. You need these more than I do," he said gently.

Remo watched through the bars as Popcorn's thin brown fingers groped for the pack. They disappeared with it and Remo lingered by the bars while Popcorn smoked in silence. For some reason, secondhand smoke seemed to suit him better these days.

The rest of the day was gray and interminable. Every head count was the same. Even Radar Dish, once night fell, did the same *Star Trek* monologue he had done earlier in the week.

After lights-out, the silence was eerie. There were no midnight howls, no night terror screams, no buzz of furtive conversation.

Everyone knew that tomorrow was Tuesday. The day Popcorn was scheduled to go to the chair. Remo wondered if the little guy would get any sleep, and then he wondered how he himself would sleep when his turn came.

He listened to Popcorn toss and turn all night and wondered if he should offer any words of comfort. Then he realized he had none. What do you tell a Dead Man as his final minutes tick by?

The morning buzzer was like a shank in the gut.

The first visitors were a pair of C.O.'s and a priest. The exchange was inaudible and one-sided. The priest soon left, his face a shocked bone-white after he realized he could not hear the condemned man's confession because he had no tongue.

Next came the barber and the warden.

Warden McSorley spoke in flat, rote-like tones over the buzz of the clippers that were whittling Popcorn's high-top fade to microscopic stubble.

"Listen carefully, Mohammed," the warden was saying. "After the barber is done, you're going to step out of your shorts and we're going to prepare your body.

Popcorn whimpered.

"Now, don't be alarmed. It's just a rubber band." The clippers stopped. "Is he done? Good. All right, Mohammed, stand up. Don't be afraid. The guard is just going to wrap the band around your penis. It's just to prevent any accidents while you're undergoing the process."

Remo shuddered at the word "process." It sounded so clinical.

"Now, bend over. Guard, insert this suppository into Mohammed's rectum. There. That wasn't so bad, was it? I'm sorry about the indignity, but it saves the undertaker a lot of unnecessary work, not having to clean the body."

Popcorn tried to speak, but all Remo could make out was a pitiful muff-muff of a sound.

"What's that?" the warden was saying in a solicitous tone. "What? Oh, yes. Customarily there is a last meal, but the doctor left specific instructions that you not eat while your tongue is stitched up like that. I'm sorry, but the doctor knows best."

"For Christ's sake," Remo exploded. "You're about to drag him off to the chair. Who gives a rat's ass if his stitches pop!"

"The person who would have to clean up the blood," the warden called back. "Guard, if that prisoner speaks out again, take him to solitary."

Remo started to tell them where they could shove solitary, but subsided, bitter that they had that to hold over him. But as they had told him the first

time he walked through the Trenton State gates, he
had forfeited his civil rights.

"All right, you may dress now," the warden went
on quietly. The rustle of clothes came next. Then the
cell door buzzed open and Remo could hear the soft
padding of Popcorn's sandaled feet on the corridor
floor. For some reason it sounded louder than the
shoes of the others.

"So long, Popcorn," a man shouted several cells
away.

"Give 'em hell, my man."

"You goin' to a better place, my man."

"Let me reassure you that the procedure is completely painless," Warden McSorley was saying as a
guard unlocked the door to the electric chair. Popcorn
whimpered miserably. He was attempting to speak,
but only an inarticulate blubbering came out.

"Catch him!" the warden shouted suddenly. "He's
collapsing."

"Don't worry, I got him. Here, let's just haul him
along."

After the commotion subsided, the hush was pal-
pable. It was a hush Remo had heard before. He was
not surprised, then, when a man walked down the
line. He wore a black hood over a simple brown
workman's uniform. He looked like a common re-
pairman.

The executioner.

After he passed Remo's cell, the wheel on the
thick door squealed shut. Then absolute silence blan-
keted the row.

The next several minutes were interminable. Remo
wondered if Popcorn was conscious when they
strapped him down. He hoped not. It seemed to take
a long time. How long could it take to strap a man
in? Remo fretted.

Then, after what seemed like forever, the lights
flickered and Remo went cold. When the flicker

came, it seemed too sudden. They flickered again. And a third time. Remo held his breath after that. Then the lights flickered a fourth and final time.

"Christ!" Remo said, sickened.

The warden reemerged, trailed by the guards and the hooded executioner.

One of the guards was saying, "Imagine that. Four jolts. And such a little squirt, too."

"Before I do this again," the executioner said testily, "I want to look that thing over again. I don't want to ever go through another one like that. I'm not up for this kind of thing. I'm semiretired, dammit!"

"I hope you feel that way when my time comes," Remo muttered sotto voce.

The executioner glanced in his direction, his eyes going wide within his leather-ringed eye holes.

He stopped, came up to Remo's cell.

"Do I know you?" he asked vaguely.

"That's a popular question lately," Remo shot back sourly.

"I *do* know you," the executioner said. "But I can't place the face."

"Yours is a blank to me," Remo said, flashing a wicked grin.

"You're a cold-blooded son of a bitch, aren't you? What's your name?"

"Look it up," Remo fired back.

"Don't worry, I will," the executioner said, and walked on.

"Guard," the warden said, "show Williams to his new cell."

"Damn! Now I've done it," Remo said bitterly, thinking he had just earned a stint in solitary.

"Williams!" the executioner said explosively. "Did you say his name was Williams?" The buzz of the control door closing cut off the warden's reply.

The guard buzzed Remo's cell open, and to Remo's surprise, he was taken to Popcorn's old cell.

"Take good care of it," the guard told him as the cell door clanged in his unhappy face. "On the row, this is the Presidential Suite."

As the guard started away, Remo called after him, "Did he die hard?"

The guard stopped. His expression was stiff. "Know what his last words were?" he asked solemnly.

"What?"

"Mumph! Mumph. Unquote." And the guard broke into howling laughter.

"He was just a kid, you bastard," Remo hissed, his knuckles whitening on the cell bars.

"Sure. A kid who blew away his own sister, left her for dead in a swamp with maggots crawling all over her."

Remo started. "What?"

"Sure. What'd he tell you?"

"That he killed his girlfriend on his birthday."

"I don't know about the birthday part, but he made a duck out of you. It was his sister, and he killed her, all right. After he raped her. But he should have read up on maggots before he poured them into her wounds. He thought they'd consume the body so it wouldn't be recognized. Instead, they ate away all the bad tissue. She was barely alive when they found her, and lingered just long enough to finger her brother. Whatever you thought of that little prick, he deserved what he got. Just as you will." The guard strode away.

Remo's eyes looked into dead space. "Son of a bitch," he muttered. "He lied to me."

Remo stumbled back to his cot and looked around. The new cell was as pink as his old one, but it smelled different. It smelled of sweat and something else, something indefinable. It smelled of fear. And cold realization hit Remo Williams.

"Damn," he muttered emptily, "I *am* next."

Remo felt very cold inside and lay back on the cot

to get a grip on himself. His hand, exploring under the pillow, encountered something soft and crushable. He pulled it out.

It was Popcorn's pack of Camels.

Remo sat up and lighted one. He took a long drag. He had less trouble this time and smoked it all the way down. As he smoked, he considered how his life had turned around. Twenty years ago, Popcorn and he would have been on opposite sides of the law. But behind bars, they had been friends of a sort.

When he was through smoking, Remo whispered into the emptiness, "Thanks, Popcorn."

12

Harold Haines felt the warden's office go dark around him. Distantly he heard Warden McSorley's voice call through the roaring in his ears.

"Haines. What is it, man? You're turning white."

The warden's voice seemed far away, so Harold Haines didn't bother to answer it. The darkness seemed to expand. All that Harold Haines saw, or cared to see, were the yellow pages of the condemned man's rap sheet in his suddenly cold hands.

"Harold?"

"It's him," Haines croaked, his eyes not wavering from the pages. "It's not just a guy with the same name. It's him. Williams."

Then the fading typed letters on the rap sheet started to jiggle uncontrollably. Harold felt himself shake. The world was a very small place as seen through the diminishing tunnel of his vision.

"Harold!"

"Haines looked up, his eyes opaque. The warden's heavy hands were on his shoulders and he was shaking Haines violently.

"Snap out of it. Here, take a chair."

Haines felt himself being guided to the hard wooden chair that except for the leather straps and copper halo was identical to the electric chair Haines had just operated. He knew this because a year ago he had salvaged an identical wooden chair from storage to serve as a replacement for the old chair, which had given out. He sat down, unmindful of the irony.

Warden McSorley towered over him, his arms folded, his care-seamed face concerned.

"This is the guy," Haines repeated. "Remo Williams."

"You said that before. And you know how it sounds. Take a deep breath and let it out slowly. Maybe the work is getting to you."

"Stop talking at me like I'm one of your god-damned cons!" Harold Haines shouted with sudden vehemence. "That man on death row shouldn't be there. He's *already* dead!"

"Nonsense. Williams is a transfer prisoner. He arrived last week from . . . well, it's in the file you're holding."

"I know. He's from Trenton State Prison, New Jersey."

McSorley showed empty hands. "There it is."

"Exactly."

"So what's the problem, Harold?"

"You don't have a con in that cell, you have a ghost."

"Harold, I've known you a long time—" McSorley began.

Haines cut him off with a curt, "Long enough to remember that until five years ago I was retired."

"Well, yes," Warden McSorley said slowly.

"I retired back around twenty years ago, when the

death penalty fell out of political favor. Forty-five years old and I was out of work. The state give me a short-money pension because after a lifetime of frying felons, they know I'm not exactly going to assimilate into another line of work. Hell, who's going to hire an execution technician? And to do what, rewire houses? So I come to Florida, live in a trailer park, and watch game shows until I start to think about wiring up my easy chair as the best way out."

"Now, Harold . . ."

"Can I finish? Thank you. I would have gone crazy, but the death-penalty thing loosened up. And even though I see the faces of the men I put down in my sleep, I offer my services to the state of Florida. The rest you know."

"Yes, the rest I know," McSorley admitted.

"One of the faces in my dreams belonged to that Williams guy," Haines snapped. "Not exactly a common name. Remo Williams. A name you'd remember. Especially if it belonged to a cop who beat a pusher to death back to Newark, New Jersey, so long ago I don't even remember the year. This rap sheet says your Remo Williams snuffed a pusher in an alley. He was a cop, too."

"You must be misremembering. You've put down . . . how many men?"

"I stopped counting long after it was too late for my peace of mind," Haines said sourly. "That guy you got in there, Warden, I did him. I remember he went easy. One jolt. And it was over. I remember feeling bad about it, too. Him being a cop once. Snuffing a pusher. What's that? Nothing. He should have gotten off. Maybe life. Never the chair. I felt sick about it for weeks after. He was one of the last guys I burned up there." Harold Haines's eyes focused in on themselves. "One of the last guys, and now he comes back to haunt me. . . ."

Warden McSorley looked at Harold Haines without comment. He took the file folder from Haines's trembling fingers and retreated to the solidity of his big desk. He flipped through the folder, reading silently.

When he was done, he laid the folder flat and placed his blunt hands atop it like a worshiper laying hands on a prayer book. His expression was thoughtful as he spoke. "We've known each other a long time, Harold. What I'm about to tell you, I will deny with my dying breath."

Haines looked up, his brown eyes hunted and dull.

"The young man you just executed, Mohammed Diladay," McSorley went on. "Do you remember remarking that we were doing him awfully soon after the last execution?"

"I think I said they were going through here like shit through a goose."

The warden winced. "Yes. Well, I'm burdened with the largest population of condemned men in the nation. I have to move them through the system as efficiently as I can. The Diladay boy would normally have had a grace period of a month after his last appeal had been turned down, except that I received a phone call from the governor urging me to expedite his execution. When I asked his honor for his reasons, he said something vague about moving the process along, which was no answer. But I recognized a certain . . . concern in his voice."

Warden McSorley paused. His lower lip crowded up around his upper lip. He went on. "I thought perhaps there was something political, even personal about his request to execute Diladay so quickly. There was really no need to hurry the process. Diladay had no chance of commutation, unless it came from the governor's own office. But now I wonder."

"You thinking what I'm thinking?" Harold Haines asked.

Warden McSorley picked up the Remo Williams file.

"Williams is next, by virtue of the state of his appeal and the time he spent on death row up in Jersey," he said thoughtfully. "It strikes me as I listen to you that perhaps the governor's concern was not with Diladay, but with Williams."

"Poor bastard. They killed him once and now they want me to do it again."

"I don't believe in ghosts, Haines. And when you settle down, you'll feel the same way, I'm sure. You may have thought you executed this man—and I believe you're sincere in that belief— but obviously you did not."

"I wonder," Harold Haines muttered.

"Hmmm?"

"Where has this guy been the last twenty years and what's he been doing that they want to kill him all over again?"

"I think I'll make a call," Warden McSorley said pointedly. He dialed the number himself after consulting a thin leather-bound directory.

"Yes, Warden Reeves, please. This is Warden McSorley down in Florida State. . . . Yes, I'll wait. . . . Hello? Sorry to bother you this early, Warden Reeves. I'd like some information about a prisoner you had up there at one time. A Remo Williams. . . . Certainly, call back anytime today."

Warden McSorley hung up. Harold Haines stood up.

"Don't you want to wait for the callback?" McSorley asked.

"I think I want to have a few words with Williams. This is driving me crazy."

"That's not wise. You'll be disturbing a condemned prisoner unnecessarily."

"If I ever want to sleep again, I gotta do this. Please, Paul."

McSorley considered silently. "Very well. I can see this has affected you deeply," he relented. "The guard will take you. Just remember, Williams knows he's the next to go. Even though his final appeal hasn't been decided on, he's apt to be on edge."

The last control door rolled shut and Harold Haines walked gingerly to the cell containing Convict Six, Remo Williams.

Williams was stretched out on his cot, his hands clasped behind his head, his eyes shut.

Harold Haines cleared his throat noisily, but the prisoner's eyes didn't open.

"I see you in my dreams," he said, his voice hoarse.

"And I see Betty Page. Go away."

"You don't understand, Williams. Your name *is* Williams, isn't it?"

"In here, I'm Convict Number Six."

"You're supposed to be dead."

"Dead Man's my other nickname. So what?"

"I executed you."

"You did a lousy job of it." Williams' voice sounded bored, but his dark eyes opened. They regarded the ceiling.

"It was a long time ago," Haines continued. "Up at Trenton. I used to work at Trenton State, where you were."

The prisoner took his time sitting up. He didn't want to show any interest, but his movements were too casual. Harold Haines knew every trick in the convict book. Williams wanted to get a closer look at him without betraying his interest. Every convict knew that once you let the man know what you wanted, he'd use it against you.

"Do you remember me?" Haines asked.

Remo's eyes bored into his. They were flat, dead-looking eyes. Bullet holes in concrete had more life in them than Williams had in his eyes. He looked older. Not twenty years older, just older. The dead eyes narrowed involuntarily.

"You look familiar, yeah," Williams said slowly. "But I don't place the face exactly."

"Up at Trenton, I wore a hood that night," Haines said tightly. "The night I pulled the switch on you. But I was the prison electrician during the day. You might have seen me around."

"Sorry."

"But I remember you real good. Where you been these last twenty years, Williams? What've you been doing?"

Remo Williams said in a voice as dead as his eyes, "Time. I've been doing time."

"Well, you ain't been doing it at Trenton State. Everybody up there knows, like I know, that you died way back when."

"You're dreaming. I'm here because I killed a guard up at Trenton. His name was . . ."

"Yeah?"

Remo's forehead wrinkled in thought. "MacCleary or something like that," he said slowly. "Yeah, MacCleary. He was hassling me. So I offed him. Now I gotta pay for it."

"I don't know if I have the stomach to fry you a second time."

Remo gave out a sad grunt of a laugh. "Don't you know?" he said airily. "Second time's the charm with guys like me."

"But you don't get it. You're *already* dead. I executed you twenty years ago!"

When, after a long time, Remo Williams said nothing in reply, Harold Haines shuffled off down the line. He felt like a Dead Man himself.

Remo Williams stared out the bars of his cell, wondering what was going on. The executioner's face had looked familiar. Where had he seen it before? And what was that crap about having been executed up at Trenton State? Remo suddenly remembered the dream of the other night. The dream in which he had been executed up at Trenton. But that was only a dream. It had never—could never have—happened.

Then the buzzer announced lunch and Remo sat up. His lungs felt like concrete. He wondered if it was the fear in his gut or the heavy cigarette smoke in his lungs. Funny how he'd been reacting to cigarettes.

Harold Haines returned to Warden McSorley's voice on leaden feet.

McSorley looked up sharply. "Have your little talk with the condemned, Harold?"

"He didn't know what I was talking about," Haines said dully.

"Well, it may not answer all your questions, but it settles some of them. If the man were dead, he'd certainly know it."

Harold Haines did not return Warden McSorley's tight smile.

The phone rang and McSorley answered it with a curt "Excuse me." Then: "Yes, Warden Reeves. . . . What's that? . . . When?" McSorley's face suddenly tightened. "I . . . I see. Actually, Warden, it was just that his name came up in a death-cell confession. Yes, I agree with you. We can't very well try a man who's already paid the state the ultimate penalty. Thank you for your time, Warden Reeves."

When Warden McSorley hung up the phone, his face was even paler than Harold Haines's running-to-fat features now.

"He's dead," McSorley said in an arid tone. "He was executed in 1971 for murdering a pusher. The Warden didn't seem aware that it was his signature on the release that transferred Williams to this facility."

Harold Haines sat up with a start. "Why don't you say something?"

"Because I value my job and my pension," Warden Paul McSorley said flatly. "I've got a man on death row who's supposed to be in his grave. I can't send him back to Trenton. They'd never accept him and they'd begin investigating. I know how these things work, believe me. Someone handed me a red-hot potato knowing if I ever found out the truth, I'd be the man with microwaved fingers."

"But what are we—you—going to do?"

"If they turn down his last appeal—and right now I'd wager my home and life savings that they do—the governor will sign his death warrant, and you, Harold, will not only carry it out, you'll never speak of this to anyone. Is that clear?"

"For God's sake!" Haines burst out. "The guy was a cop once. He was on our side."

"According to his sheet, he killed a prison guard named Conrad MacCleary in cold blood. I don't know what's real here and what's not, but I'm simply going to do my job and I strongly urge you to do the same. We're not young men, either of us. We know how the world works. Let's deal with this unpleasantness as quietly and quickly as good public servants and get on with the rest of our lives. Now, I expect you'll want to go home, Harold. You killed a man today and you look like you could use a stiff belt."

"I don't drink. You know that. I gave it up when I felt myself sliding into the bottle."

"Harold," Warden McSorley said, handing him a file, "I'd give alcoholism a second look were I you. Now, please excuse me. And take this with you. On your way out, ask my secretary to kindly return it to Central Files."

Harold Haines took the file marked "Remo Williams" and closed the door behind him silently.

13

George Proctor perspired in the stupefying Florida heat as he left his parked car and approached the prison gatehouse, which, except for its pastel green coloring and lack of a sign, might have been a forgotten Fotomat booth.

"Business?" a guard wearing mirrored sunglasses inquired in a laconic voice.

"The usual," Proctor said, flashing his ID. "Client."

"Pass on through," the guard said, signaling to the booth. Another guard hit a switch and the tall fence rolled back on creaky casters. Proctor stepped through the opening, thinking that today's business was anything but usual.

It had started with an appearance before a judge at the Florida Supreme Court—a judge known to be sympathetic to death-row appeals. The judge had gaveled the appeal down so fast that George Proctor was halfway down the courthouse steps, briefs in hand, before it dawned on him that the telephone call he had received the night before was no prank. That, and the judge's uncharacteristic coldness, were somehow related.

Proctor entered the main doors and identified himself for the guard in the cramped control booth and was escorted through the growing din and into the conference room. After a brief wait, Remo Williams was brought in.

He sat down with an even deader look to his eyes

than before. Proctor had wondered why those eyes had seemed so familiar before. Now, seeing Williams again, he thought he understood. The man had cop eyes. The flat expressionless eyes that come to police officers after too many years of seeing too much of society's dark underbelly. Proctor never connected that flicker of recognition with the artist's drawing he had seen in a supermarket-checkout-line tabloid. He never read those rags—except when the person ahead of him paid with a check. And then he always put the things back unpurchased.

"It's not good, is it?" Williams asked in a voice as dead as his eyes.

"The State Supreme Court turned us down." Proctor emphasized the word "us" to let Williams think they were in this together. In fact, he had already decided this would be their last meeting.

"Then you're going up to the Supreme Court."

Proctor couldn't lie. He took a deep breath. "I have to be honest with you, Williams," he said. "I did file, but I don't think I can continue with this case."

Remo's eyes tightened. "What?"

"Look, I don't know what's going on," Proctor said miserably, "but I put this before Justice Hannavan, and he turned me down cold. The guy is an incurable softy." Proctor looked around the room before speaking, even though it was empty but for a single out-of-earshot guard. "I . . . I think they got to him."

"They? Who?"

Proctor leaned forward, his eyes on the wooden-faced C.O. Even though this conversation fell under the client-confidentiality statutes, he dropped his voice.

"The same ones that got you transferred to this state," he said. "The ones who called me last night."

"Be straight with me. Who?"

"I don't know who, but they have to be connected

on the federal level. I was warned that I had been videotaped doing cocaine at a party."

"Oh, that's just peachy," Remo said. "My lawyer, the cokehead."

"It was only a line. Maybe two," Proctor said quickly. "Strictly recreational. But they're threatening to slap me with a possession-with-intent-to-sell beef. But I'm innocent. Really!"

"You sound like a con," Remo said nastily.

"I feel like a political prisoner, Williams. This is scary police-state stuff. Someone wants you dead. And they want you dead yesterday. I had no sooner left the hearing than I received notice that the governor had signed your death warrant. I filed for a stay with the U.S. Supreme Court and got us a short date."

"For when?"

"The day after tomorrow."

"What do you think our chances are?"

"Not great. Your excecution is set for tomorrow morning."

Proctor steeled himself for the ex-cop's reaction. He didn't know what to expect. Remo's cop eyes seemed to recede into his head. Actually, it was an illusion caused by a slight bowing of the man's head. The overhead light threw his socket hollows into shadow, making them look like skull holes.

I'm looking at a dead man, Proctor thought, suddenly chilled. Poor bastard.

"They can't execute before the appeal is decided," Williams said quietly, not looking up. "Can they?"

"Normally, no. But in this case, I don't know. Look, I'm sorry, I shouldn't even be telling you any of this, but I would lose my practice if I took an intent-to-sell fall. And for what? A pro bono appeal that was dumped in my lap? Put yourself in my place. What would *you* do?"

"Put yourself in *my* place," Remo said between

set teeth. "What would you expect from *your* lawyer?"

"I'm sorry. I really am."

"The least you could do is refer me to another lawyer," Remo grated. "Fast!"

"That's the other thing," Proctor added. "I called your former lawyer, hoping to dump this on him. I got a delicatessen. I redialed, figuring I had misread the letterhead, and got the same place. I checked with the Jersey bar. The man who represented you went out of business twelve years ago. He's been dead four."

"Impossible. I saw him only last . . . month. I think."

"Not unless there are two of him. For God's sake, Williams, who are you? Nobody gets railroaded like this. It wouldn't surprise me if they had the Supreme Court rigged."

"I'm Remo Williams," Remo said vaguely. "Aren't I?"

"If you don't know, who would?"

George Proctor watched as his client seemed to shrink in his tight-fitting apricot T-shirt. His eyes were staring down at his hands, which lay flat on the counter in front of the glass partition. He looked calm—calmer than Proctor thought he had any right to look.

"He said he had already killed me," Williams intoned without looking up.

"Who?"

Williams raised his face, his eyes bleak. "The executioner. They buried Popcorn this morning."

"I have no idea what you're babbling about."

"Mohammed Diladay. They called him Popcorn. He was executed this morning."

"That's odd. There was no press coverage."

"The executioner walked by my cell," Remo went on. "He did a double-take. Said something about having executed me up in Trenton State twenty years ago."

"You're not making this up, are you? I mean, it's a little late for an insanity plea."

"A few nights ago," Remo went on as if talking to himself, "I dreamed that I had been executed. At Trenton. It seemed real. And for some reason, the executioner's face looked familiar."

"Oh, Christ!" Proctor said hoarsely. He grabbed up his valise hastily.

"What does that tell you?" Williams asked tightly.

"It tells me that I should get the fuck out of here. Sorry, Williams. You have my sympathy. But I want no part of you."

"What about my rights? What about the law?"

"A few years ago I would have fought this tooth and nail, believe me. But I've got a wife now. Two kids. A condo. I get jammed up, she'll leave me and take the kids with her. I'm not an idealistic young guy anymore. Sorry. Good-bye."

Remo Williams watched his last hope in the world walk off in a six-hundred-dollar suit, his insides feeling like chopped liver too long in the refrigerator. He didn't hear the door behind him open and the guard shouting his name.

"Williams!" the guard repeated, taking him by the arm.

Remo tensed, nearly jumped to his feet and down the guard's open throat. Then his eyes refocused and, head bowed, he allowed himself to be led back to his cell.

His biggest regret was that Popcorn wasn't there to talk to. Already he missed the little con. But on this, the last day of his life, he had no interest in trying to start up a new friendship through pink cinder block.

Remo thought back to the night his fellow officers

came to his apartment and apologetically informed him he was under arrest for the murder of a black drug pusher whose name, over twenty years later, Remo could no longer remember. An important fact like that, and he couldn't summon it up. The judge and the prosecution must have repeated it a thousand times throughout the trial. What was the judge's name? Harold something. Smith, that was it. Smith. A sourpuss, with his starchy white hair and puritanical mouth. The guy had worn rimless glasses, so he looked like a high-school headmaster gone old and sour.

"Wait a minute," Remo blurted out. "That face!" Suddenly he remembered. Judge Harold Smith. That was the face in one of his strange dreams. What did it mean?

Dinner was spaghetti with meatballs. Remo refused it. His appetite had fled.

"You sure?" the guard had asked. It was the one who had questioned him over the *National Enquirer* article the other day. His name tag said: Fletcher. "I hear this could be your last supper."

"Then it's true," Remo said, hollow-voiced.

"They're keeping mum about it. But that's the buzz. Pardon the expression."

"Look, I don't want the food. But you can do me a favor."

"And I could lose my job," the guard said, his voice going from solicitous to crystal hard in midsyllable.

"It's nothing illegal," Remo assured him. "You had a newspaper the other day. It had my face on it. How about letting me have it, huh? Just something to read, to take my mind off my troubles."

The guard hesitated. He rubbed his undershot jaw thoughtfully. "Can't see that it'll do any harm," he admitted. "Just do me a favor. After you're done

with it, shove it under the mattress. I'll get it after
. . . you know."

"It's a promise," Remo said as the guard snatched
up the tray from the cell-door slot.

Remo had to wait until the guard was finished
feeding the row before he wandered back. His first
words made Remo's heart sink.

"I checked the prison library," he said. "Couldn't
find it. But the new one came in." He stuffed the
folded paper into the slot. Remo had to use both
hands to wrestle it through without tearing it to
pieces.

"That do?" the guard asked.

"Yeah," Remo said as his eye caught sight of the
headline STARTLING FURTHER RELEVATIONS OF "DEAD
MAN."

"Remember that promise," the guard said, walking off.

"Sure, no problem," Remo said vaguely, folding
open the front page. There was a reproduction of the
earlier artist's sketch of his face. It looked like a
police I.D. sketch, but beside it was another sketch.
This one was of a wizened old Asian man with a wisp
of a beard hanging from his chin, and clear, penetrat-
ing eyes.

In a box beside that face was the following: "First
Look at Dead Man's Spirit Guide, Identified by
Enquirer Panel of Psychics as Lim Ting Tong, High
Priest of the Lost Continent of Mu. See Page 7."

Remo, reading this, sank onto his cot heavily. The
face of the old Asian was identical to the face from
his dream. The one called Chiun. Swiftly Remo turned
to page 7. He read so fast his eyes skipped over
whole sentences as he searched for his own name.
He found it.

The gist of the article was that *Enquirer* readers
from across the country had written in to share sightings of Dead Man, who had been brought to the

Enquirer's attention by renowned University of Massachusetts anthropology professor Naomi Vanderkloot. According to Vanderkloot, Dead Man, by virtue of his superhuman feats, could be none other than the vanguard of the next evolution in *Homo sapiens*.

Enquirer readers had come forward with their own accounts, many of which agreed that Dead Man was often accompanied by an old Oriental in colorful robes. No one knew Dead Man's true name. Or at least no one could agree upon it. A Detroit hotel manager had identified him as a former guest of his establishment who had signed the register book "Remo Murray." A Malibu boat dealer claimed that "Remo Robeson" had purchased a Chinese junk from him only last year and sailed away in it. And on and on the reports went, some sightings going back over a dozen years. All the reports agreed that the man's first name was Remo. The last name was always different. "Williams" was not one of the examples.

"My name," Remo Williams muttered in the reflected pink glow of his bare cell. "My face. But how could I be in two places at once—in prison and out on the street?"

Remo read the article over and over until he knew it by heart. Then he stuffed it under the mattress.

Lights-out came and Remo didn't bother undressing or getting under the covers. Tomorrow at seven A.M. he would walk down the line, not for the killing he hadn't committed over twenty years ago, but for the murder of a Trenton guard he had been forced to kill only because he had been sent up for a killing he never did in the first place. The guard had been an asshole. He had asked for it, Remo thought, but he was a corrections officer. The irony was that after fighting to escape death row for someone else's crime, Remo Williams was about to pay the ultimate price for one he was forced to commit.

Remo replayed the killing over and over in his

mind. He remembered sticking the makeshift shank in the man's stomach and "jugging" it—twisting the rusty blade to maximize the internal damage. It replayed like a continuous loop film strip. He didn't realize he was drifting off to sleep.

Remo dreamed. He was walking down a long tree-lined country road. The fog hung low, as if in an old Universal horror movie. Up ahead, the wrought-iron gates of a sprawling brick complex loomed. In his dream, Remo thought it was a prison, but as he approached, he saw the brass plate gleam against a stone pillar topped by a severe lion's head.

It read: FOLCROFT SANITARIUM.

The gates were padlocked. Remo leapt for them anxiously.

"Let me in," Remo cried, rattling the chain. He pulled on the fence. It rattled too, but wouldn't budge. "Can anyone hear me? They're coming to get me."

A splash of headlights illuminated him from behind. A long car turned the corner, its wheels lost in fog. It was a hearse. A white hearse. Remo attacked the fence with renewed ferocity.

"Someone answer me! Please!" he cried.

And through the mists on the other side of cell-like fence floated a figure in saffron robes. The old Oriental. Not Lim Ting Tong. His name was Chiun and he pointed at Remo with stern, long-fingered nails.

"Go back, white. I deny you. Never again will you enter these hallowed halls."

"It's me. Remo. Don't you know me?"

"I know you too well," Chiun intoned. "You have shamed me. Forever. I can bear to look upon your disgraceful form no longer."

"But why? What did I do?"

"Your elbow." The voice rumbled like doom.

"What about it?" Remo said anxiously. Car doors slammed behind him. He was afraid to look back over his shoulder.

"It was bent!" The Oriental's words dripped bitterness.

And then, materializing from the mists was a tall vulturelike figure in black robes. Not an Oriental kimono, but a judge's funereal robes. The figure looked at Remo with a disapproving expression on his dry-as-dust features. Remo recognized the face. Judge Harold Smith.

"He refuses to leave us alone," the Oriental told Smith.

"Remo Williams," the judge pronounced, "I have sentenced you to death." Smith pointed beyond Remo.

Remo turned. The white hearse was parked with its rear gate to him. It was open, and inside was a legless electric chair. And standing beside it, attired in a three-piece gray suit, was the executioner, his head smothered in a black leather hood.

"Who are you?" Remo demanded.

The executioner's voice was chilly. "You know me. We have done this before."

Impelled by some irresistible urge he could not explain, Remo approached the executioner.

"Please take a seat," the executioner said solemnly. His feet were enveloped by low-lying ground fog, like a ghost.

"I know your voice," Remo said. Impulsively he reached for the hood. It came away, leaving the craggy, soft features of Harold Haines. But there was something wrong with the face. It didn't match the voice. Remo pulled at the man's suddenly obvious false nose. The face came away, and the hair. A mask. And behind it were the austere features of Judge Harold Smith.

"No!" Remo shrank from Smith's cold, unhuman eyes. He made a break for the gate. The old Oriental

bounded to intecept him. He took the gates in his
tiny hands as if to hold them in place against Remo's
assault.

Remo shouted in mid-course, feeling the ground
pushing against his running toes. He ran into the
stone wall and up the side, his toes shifting from the
soft horizontal ground to the hard vertical wall as
easily as from sand to blacktop.

At the top, Remo paused, read the distance to the
ground, and jumped. He floated to the grass as if
weightless. Remo ran past the old Oriental, away
from Judge Harold Smith's grasping hands, and into
the building. An elevator took him to the second
floor and the door marked DIRECTOR. Remo pushed
the door in.

A man sat in a cracked leather chair behind a
Spartan oak desk. The chair was turned to a big
picture window that framed a large body of water, so
that only the back of the man's head was visible over
the high seat back. His hair was white.

Then the chair slowly swiveled and the sharp pro-
file came into view, continued until the shaky fluorescent lights made the round rimless eyeglasses
momentarily opaque, and then the gray eyes looked
at him reprovingly.

Remo's eyes jumped to the nameplate: "Harold
W. Smith, Director."

Without a word, Smith pressed an intercom button and suddenly Remo was surrounded by burly
orderlies in hospital green. They grabbed Remo by
the arms and the legs and wrestled him to the floor,
trying to force his arms into a straitjacket. Only after
they had succeeded in locking Remo into the strangling garment did he see the electrical connectors on
the jacket front. Then, to his horror, they were pushing into the office a complicated electronic device on
a wheeled stand. Swiftly, grimly, they plugged heavy
old-fashioned jacks into the connectors, and the voice

of Harold W. Smith, as astringent and pitiless as lemon dishwater detergent, was asking Remo a doleful question. "Do you have any last words?"

His last word was to scream the name "Chiun" in an anguished voice. And then a grinning orderly threw an antiquated knife-switch.

"What's wrong?" Smith asked over Remo's howl of fear.

"The damned jacks," the orderly barked. "We connected them wrong. Have to try again."

"Do it!"

Remo snapped awake. He was breathing like a drowning man. He couldn't see past the cold sweat that dripped down his forehead and into his eyes. His T-shirt was soaked. And cold. It stuck to his skin.

Remo rolled out of bed. None of it made sense, but it was adding up in a weird way. Dreams and reality. They were mixed up in his mind. What was real? What was it Popcorn had said? Dead Men dream deepest.

After Remo got a grip on himself, he walked over to the cell door. He placed his fingers against the electronic lock. It had worked in the dream. He started tapping. He felt foolish as he varied the rhythm of his fingers. He closed his eyes, trying to remember exactly how it worked in the dream.

Almost at once, he felt something. A current, a vibration. He keyed into it like a concert pianist playing a half-forgotten chord.

Miraculously, the door rolled aside. Remo stepped out into the corridor. He walked low, keeping to the far wall. The lights were out, which made it easier. He came to the first section-control door, found the lock with his fingers, and started tapping. He crouched under the glass window of the door.

The door rolled aside. There were no guards visible beyond.

A gasp came from a cell. Another man snored. A third crept to his cell bars for a better look. Remo met his eyes in the darkness.

The man shot Remo a thumbs-up sign and said, "Good luck, Dead Man."

Remo nodded and moved to the next door.

Beyond the third door was a control booth. Remo peered up and saw that the guard on duty was sitting behind the Plexiglas reading a newspaper. His face was turned toward the corridor. But Remo had gotten this far. He had to go on.

The door rolled open after a brief manipulation. Remo froze, exposed. In a dream, he remembered Chiun's exortation to stay still whenever he was within range of a man's peripheral vision. Remo waited till the guard finished the paper and looked up. The door had rolled shut automatically, and only when the guard was staring directly at him through almost impenetrable darkness did Remo advance on him.

For some reason, Remo could see through the darkness like a gray haze. He moved on the booth like a jungle cat stalking, feeling the freedom in his muscles, feeling something else he hadn't felt since the day he woke up on Florida's death row: confidence.

Remo saw that the only door to the booth was on the other side of the wall. There was no way in from this corridor.

He decided on the bold approach and walked right up to the glass. Remo knocked on the Plexiglas. The guard jumped nearly a foot.

Remo smiled at him disarmingly, as if nothing was wrong. He opened his mouth and made shapes with it, but no words. The guard's "What?" was dim but audible through the Plexiglas.

Remo repeated his pantomime, pointing back toward the row.

The guard gave him a terse, "Wait a minute," and stepped through the exit door. Remo waited tensely.

A corridor door rolled back and the guard hurried in, demanding, "What is it?"

Remo decked him with a sharp fist to the jaw. Swiftly he stripped the guard and exchanged pants with him. He donned his jacket over his apricot T-shirt. Then he ducked back, not bothering to hide the body. He knew that the quickest way out was through Grand Central, and beyond that, the yard. It was also the most dangerous way out of the facility.

Walking with an easy grace, Remo moved from door to door, until he was in the cathedrallike Grand Central. The tiers of C Block towered above him like medieval dungeons designed by a condo-mentality architect.

He kept to the shadows until he got to the door leading to the yard. It gave under his tapping fingers and Remo found himself on the threshold of the yard, and freedom.

Out there, the lights were too bright for shadows to exist. He took a deep breath.

Confidently Remo stepped out, knowing that his guard uniform would buy him a minute. Maybe more than a minute.

He got only four paces when a searchlight swiveled in his direction. Remo shielded his face with an upraised forearm, a natural eye-protecting gesture that also concealed his identity.

"Who goes there!" a voice called down.

"It's me!" Remo said in a gargling voice. "Pepone."

"What's the problem, Pepone?"

"Dead Man on the loose. We got him cornered in the shower room. Warden says to watch the outside walls for a car or accomplice."

"Right," the guard returned. The searchlight obligingly swiveled out of Remo's eyes and began to rake the grass beyond the fence.

Remo stepped back into the exit door, and then, after a pause, he sprinted out for the wall.

He ran stiffly at first, and then something in him
clicked over. He hit the inner fence like a monkey
going up, vaulting over the razor wire to drop to the
narrow dirt corridor between it and the outer fence.
He raced to the outer fence. A bullet spanked a rock
beside his shoes.

"Halt!" an emotion-charged voice ordered.

Remo knew that the guards had standing shoot-to-
kill orders—his uniform notwithstanding—for anyone caught where he was now. Going up the fence
was suicide, so he went through the fence. He didn't
think about what he was doing. It was as if his body
was on autopilot. His hands took hold of fistfuls of
chain link until he had a group that felt soft. He
twisted violently. To his astonishment, the fence un-
raveled vertically, like a poorly knit sweater.

Remo dashed through the opening. Shots cracked
behind him. No one came close. He ran zigzag fash-
ion, the way he had been taught in the Marines.
Distantly a shotgun boomed once. Twice.

Remo grinned wolfishly. He knew shotguns. At
this range, the guard could shove the close-range
weapon up his own ass for all the good it would do
him.

Remo could hear the cars starting up. The gate
was ordered opened. Electric motors hummed as the
gates rolled aside. The escapee warning siren started
yowling.

In the darkness, Remo doubled back. They would
never expect that. He eased into the shelter of the
gatehouse as one of the two guards on duty ran out,
rifle in hand, and hopped into the first patrol car
tearing out of the gate.

While a procession of cars roared out and the siren
wailed from the control tower, Remo slipped into the
guard box and up behind the unsuspecting guard.
He took the man's throat in both hands and squeezed
until the blood to the brain was choked off long

enough to cause unconsciousness. He couldn't remember where he'd learned that trick, but as he lowered the man's limp body to the floor, it was obvious he'd learned it well.

Remo waved to the cars as they continued spitting out of the prison gates. Hours later, after they still had not returned and dawn was a smoky red crack on the eastern horizon, Remo casually picked up a workman's lunchbox and walked up the prison road as if going home after a long night of work.

None of the tower guards bothered him. In his black and gray guard's uniform he was virtually invisible.

It was the morning before his execution, but Remo felt, for the first time in a long time, like a free man.

His first order of business, he decided, was to find out how long that had really been. . . .

14

The Master of Sinanju sat in the House of the Masters, surrounded by the yellowing scrolls of his ancestors.

Somewhere in these histories, inscribed by hand by one of his ancestors—the guardians of the House of Sinanju—there must be a hint or clue as to how to deal with the problem of Remo.

Chiun sighed. After many days of careful study, he had not found the answer he had returned to Sinanju to seek. It would have been so much easier to blame this on Remo's whiteness. He was the first white

ever to be trained in the art of Sinanju. His foreign
birth, his mongrel heritage, excused much of what
was wrong with Remo Williams, his pupil and the
only heir to the Sinanju tradition other than Chiun
himself.

No, this problem with Remo was that he fulfilled
the prophecy of Shiva. His weaknesses were his
strengths. The very thing that made him worthy of
Sinanju was the thing that now threatened not only
to tear him from Chiun but also to smash irrevocably
the proud line that was the House of Sinanju, which
stretched back into the mists of antiquity.

Tiredly Chiun gathered up the parchment scrolls.
He would study them later, for soon he must go
down the shore road and treat with the waiting vessel of the Americans.

As Chiun floated to his sandaled feet, there came a
timid knocking at the door to his chambers. Girding
his skirts, he spoke up in a tone befitting a Master of
Sinanju.

"Who dares disturb my study?" he demanded.

"It is I, Pullyang," a quavering old voice replied.
"Your faithful servant,"

"It had better be important," Chiun warned.

"Two round-eyed whites stand on our sand, O
Master. They come from the iron fish. They bear
an important message for you."

Chiun leapt to the door, but measured his strides
so that it would not seem to his faithful caretaker that
he was in an unseemly hurry to meet with the
Americans.

"Fortunately, you have come at a time when I
could do with a walk," Chiun said importantly as he
stepped out of the room.

Pullyang, bent with age, a cold reed pipe in one
hand, executed a full bow at Chiun's approach, getting down on all fours and touching the floor with his
forehead.

"I will carry word of your approach to them," Pullyang said.

"No. There is no need to expose yourself to their ugly big-nosed, round-eyed faces again. I will deal with them. No doubt they seek a boon, which I will of course deny them. Whites. They are forever seeking my wisdom. Sometimes even autographs."

"What are autographs?" Pullyang stumbled over the unfamiliar foreign word as they emerged from the House of the Masters.

"White Americans value them very highly," Chiun replied as he stepped down the hill to the water. "Yet they are merely the names of unimportant personages written on scraps of paper."

"The ways of the outside world are those of the mad."

"Agreed," said Chiun, outpacing old Pullyang without seeming to hurry. It was several hours before the agreed-upon contact time. Chiun wondered if word had come from his emperor.

They reached the beach, where two men stood shivering in silence.

"Greetings, emissaries of Harold the Generous," Chiun told the two seamen. They stood beside a beached rubber craft. They exchanged uncomprehending glances at Chiun's salutation. Obviously they were mental defectives, like most who earned their livelihood by crossing the ocean's face instead of fishing from it.

"Our skipper asked that we deliver this to you," one said, offering a square of paper.

Chiun accepted the envelope. It was sealed. Inside was a thin sheet of yellow paper. The machine-typed message was short:

Chiun:
Vacation Extended Indefinitely. Do Not Return Until Contacted. R.W.'s Undercover Assignment

Taking Longer Than Anticipated. Await Further Contact.

The Director

Chiun's wizened face puckered so that his wrinkles appeared to radiate even more wrinkles. He looked up at the seaman with clear, guileless eyes.

"This urgent message commands me to return to America at once," he said brusquely.

"We're ready to ferry you back to the boat, sir."

"One moment," Chiun said, turning to the shore road, where Pullyang hung back, watching with unabashed curiosity.

"Faithful Pullyang," Chiun called up in Korean. "Have the strongest men of the village bring me my green trunk. And then seal the House of the Masters. I am returning to America this very hour."

"But what of the villagers?" Pullyang said unhappily. "Will there be no farewell feast?"

"Inform my people," Chiun said, eyeing the Americans for any hint that they understood his tongue, "that if they wish the Master of Sinanju to provide them with a feast, they had better show him more appreciation in the future."

Pullyang departed in haste.

Chiun turned to the American seamen and he smiled placidly. "My luggage is being brought to this very spot," he explained in their sparse, unlovely language. "Then we must depart as quickly as possible. If my faithful villagers learn that I am leaving them so soon, they will shriek and rend their garments and put up all manner of commotion to persuade me to remain, for they love me greatly—I, who am the center of the universe to them."

"Maybe we should take you now and come back for your things," one of the seamen suggested earnestly, while the other cast uneasy glances out over the West Korea Bay.

"No, it will only be a moment," said Chiun, cocking a delicate shell ear for the sound of shrieking and garment-rending. Hearing nothing of the sort, he lapsed into a sullen silence. Had the people of Sinanju sunk into such ingratitude that they were going to embarrass him in front of the Americans by allowing him to take his leave without begging and pleading?

15

Harold Haines drove through the predawn darkness from his Starke, Florida, home with the bleary eyes of a man who had not slept. He had not. He popped caffeine pills to keep himself awake as the twin funnels of his headlights burrowed through the thick hot air.

In less than seventeen hours he would press a button and monitor the three meters, one marked "Head," the others marked "Right Leg" and "Left Leg," that monitored the amperes going through each electrode to the condemned man, repeating the process as many times as it took for the attending physician to pronounce him dead.

Harold Haines intended to spend all day making certain that only one press of the button would be necessary.

This would be the last one, Haines decided. No more. He had electrocuted more than his share of men. And for what? Florida only paid one hundred and fifty dollars per subject. It wasn't worth this. He felt . . . burnt out. That was the only word for it.

Burnt out. Just like the men who had sat on the hot seat. Only Harold Haines still lived.

A few more hours. And he would retire for good. The only reason he didn't quit immediately, he told himself, was that Remo Williams represented unfinished business. As much as he felt no stomach to cook him again, he was more afraid not to. He didn't understand why. He was a professional execution technician. People in his line of work couldn't afford to be superstitious. And he had never had a superstitious thought in his life.

Tonight, Harold Haines felt haunted.

The road twisted ahead. It was like driving through hot, sodden cotton. He put another bitter caffeine pill in his mouth and swallowed it dry. His eyes held the road with difficulty.

And then, so suddenly that it was like a materialization, a lean man emerged from the side of the road, waving a C.O.'s jacket. A man wearing gray-striped guard pants and the apricot T-shirt of the row.

"Oh, Jesus!" Harold Haines cried. He hit the accelerator. The man leapt into his headlights and vanished.

"It's him!" Haines moaned. "Williams. My God, I ran over him."

Haines hit the brakes and his car fishtailed wildly, scattering the roadside palmetto bugs, swapped ends, and came to a stop, its grille pointing away from the prison, not far distant in the suffocating night.

Harold Haines stumbled from his car. His headlights impaled the dirt road with insect-busy illumination. He couldn't see a body. Maybe he hadn't hit him after all. There hadn't been any impact sound. Unless the guy went under the chassis and between the wheels. Haines's mind flashed back to an incident many years ago when he had run over a cat.

The cat had unexpectedly leapt from a roadside hedge, directly in the path of Haines's car. There had been no place to swerve on the narrow one-way road. The cat—it was a common tabby—disappeared under his bumper. No crush of bones. No thud of impact.

In his rearview mirror Harold Haines had seen the cat rolling in the wake of his car, apparently unharmed. He pulled over and ran back to the poor creature. It was on its back, its paws shaking violently, as if it were warding off an unseen predator.

Carefully, because it looked so helpless, Harold Haines used his shoe to nudge the agitated feline to the curb and out of the way of oncoming traffic. It stopped squirming when it nudged the curb. But its paws continued that spasmodic frantic twitching. And then the blood began to seep from its open, silent mouth. Only then did Harold Haines realize it was dying—or dead, its brain neurons causing that furious electric spasming.

Many years ago, but as fresh as the palmetto bugs that scurried from his path.

As Harold Haines loped down the road, he half-expected to see the condemned man lying in the dirt, on his back, his eyes wide and unseeing, his arms and legs twisting violently like . . . like an electrocution victim's.

Instead, an apricot-hued flash came upon him in the darkness to chop him down with the hard edge of a hand to the side of Harold Haines's thick neck. He went down hard. He didn't know he twitched until he woke up—he had no inkling how much later—to find himself alone in the dark, his car gone, his hands and feet working jerkily, as if fighting off an aerial predator.

Harold Haines dragged himself to the side of the road and sobbed quietly. When he found his courage, he began a stubborn lope to the gates of Florida State Prison.

Haines was allowed through the gate by a tight-lipped C.O.

"I was ambushed," he told the guard. "Williams. He must have escaped."

"We know. See the warden. Right now."

Warden McSorley was on the phone when Harold Haines was brought into his office. McSorley waved him to a seat impatiently and turned his attention back to his call.

"Yes, Governor. I *do* understand, Governor. But we can't hush something like this up. He was scheduled for execution"—McSorley looked at his watch—"excuse me, *is* scheduled to walk down the line exactly two hours from now."

McSorley listened in silence for so long Harold Haines was forced to pop another caffeine pill. He was starting to feel light-headed. He tried to follow the conversation from the warden's side, and although the words were clear, Haines was still not receiving. His fingertips vibrated like harp strings.

When McSorley finally put down the telephone, he hit an intercom button and spoke to his secretary.

"Tell the watch commander to call off the search. No, no explanation. But I want the entire facility to remain on lockdown until we find out how the prisoner escaped."

Then McSorley looked up with tired eyes.

"Looks like you don't work today, Harold," he said.

"I quit," Harold Haines returned dully.

"I may join you. I had the most peculiar conversation with the governor. He told me in no uncertain terms not to pursue Williams. He escaped. I guess you know."

"He ambushed my car. Stole it."

"I wish you hadn't told me that. Look, Harold, I don't know what this is about. I may end up being hung out to dry, politically, but the governor said to abandon the search and make sure no word of this leaks. He wouldn't say why. Can I count on you?"

"I'm afraid," Haines said sincerely. His fingers twined like mating worms.

"Of what?"

"He's gonna come back to get me," Harold Haines said, burying his head in his hands. "I just know he is. You should have seen his eyes in the headlights. They were like tiger eyes. They glowed. His eyes were dead, but they glowed."

"Put it out of your mind," McSorley said, rising. "Whoever or whatever that boy is—or was—he's well on his way out of Florida and I doubt that he's ever coming back. Now, if you'll excuse me, I have to go down to Central Files, personally burn the Remo Williams file, and spit on the ashes."

16

Outside Charleston, South Carolina, Remo Williams' stolen car ran out of gas. He coasted it to a stop in the breakdown lane of Route 95 North.

There was no point in putting up the hood as a distress signal. Remo had no I.D., no driver's license, no registration, and no money. And for all he knew, the state police had been alerted to his description. Although he was starting to wonder about that. He had encountered no roadblocks leaving Florida, no cruising state police in Georgia. It seemed too easy.

Remo left the car and started walking backward, his thumb hooked hitchhiker-style. He didn't expect to be offered a ride and was not disappointed. He was waiting for the first long-haul truck to come his way.

An eighteen-wheeler eventually rumbled up, and Remo, not thinking that what he was about to attempt was dangerous, if not impossible, leapt into the wake of its exhaust. He caught the tailgate in his hands and levered himself into sitting on it with a twisting spring of his feet. It was that easy.

Remo sat perched on the tailgate, watching the following cars. He was still too conspicuous. He tried the locking lever of the truck gate. It creaked open. Remo let the folding gate rise enough to admit him, and rolled inside.

The truck interior smelled of oranges. They reminded Remo that he was hungry. After pulling down the gate, he broke open a wooden crate and began peeling a dozen oranges with his hard fingers. He ate intently. Then Remo found a clear space and fell asleep, grateful for his full stomach and his life. He was living on borrowed time now, but all he cared about was sleep.

The truck stopped several times along the way, but the cargo door wasn't opened. The stink of diesel exhaust began to be a problem. Remo was having trouble breathing.

Although the darkness of the truck interior didn't seem to change, Remo could sense, somehow, that night had fallen. The truck was rumbling along, speeding up and slowing down as the driver managed the fast flow of superhighway traffic. Remo hoped the truck was continuing north.

He knew that there was more to the chain of events that had buffeted him since he woke up at Florida State than he understood. The answers, he felt, were somehow connected with a place called Folcroft Sanitarium.

The trouble was, he had no idea where Folcroft Sanitarium was—or if it actually existed.

But finding the University of Massachusetts and an anthropology professor named Naomi Vanderkloot should be no great challenge. . . .

The drone of the eighteen wheels put Remo to sleep again.

17

In his office overlooking Long Island Sound, the director of Folcroft Sanitarium watched as the cursor raced back and forth on the desktop computer screen, making phosphorescent green letters like a high-speed snail laying a trail of slime.

There were no reports of a man answering the description of the escaped death-row inmate Remo Williams coming in from any of the usual sources. A man like Williams was unpredictable. But without money or identification, he shouldn't get very far.

The director leaned back in the chair, which was so old it felt like the springs would break under the pressure of his weight. He steepled his tented fingers under his chin and half-closed his eyes in thought.

"Now, where would I go were I he?" he said aloud. "The man has no home, no relatives, no friends. He cannot come here, therefore Folcroft is safe."

His eyes darted to a new line appearing on the computer screen. It was some errant nonsense about a security threat emanating from the Chinese embassy in Washington. Time enough for such matters later.

"Perhaps he will flee the country," the director of Folcroft mused. "Perhaps that would not be a problem. He disappears. He was meant to disappear. Europe is not as final as the grave, but it is sufficient for my immediate needs."

His small lips pursed unhappily, shrinking to an obscene wet sphincter.

"No. Too untidy," he said after a time. "Where would he go? Where *could* he go?" Possibly not ordering an all-points bulletin was a mistake, after all. But Remo Williams officially did not exist. Putting out a nationwide alert for his apprehension would raise more questions than it would answer. It was fortunate that among the networks of informers he controlled, one was a guard at Florida State Prison who believed he was actually feeding criminal intelligence to the FBI branch office in Miami. His monthly bonus check ensured that he would continue to do so. It had been the guard who had tipped off the FBI—or so he believed—of the escape of the prisoner named Remo Williams in the predawn hours.

The director of Folcroft had moved swiftly. He had phoned the Florida governor and applied the requisite pressure to have the state simply ignore the jailbreak. It was an extraordinary demand, but this was an extraordinary circumstance. Fortunately the governor had a skeleton in his closet, according to the Folcroft data base. A very exploitable skeleton. It would have ruined his aspirations to higher office. He had been most compliant in the matter of Remo Williams, a seemingly unimportant death-row inmate who should have been put down decades ago.

But containing this situation was not the same as managing it to a successful conclusion. He must locate Williams.

"Where would he go?" he repeated softly. His watery eyes stared at the shininess of his well-manicured fingernails. "Where?"

Another line of text appeared on the computer screen. It lengthened. He waited until the readout was complete before reading it.

It was a follow-up to the prison-guard informant's report. Contraband reading material had been discovered under the escaped convict's mattress. An investigation was under way. The contraband was the current edition of the *National Enquirer*.

The director of Folcroft Sanitarium's thick hand raced to the top desk drawer. There, folded neatly, were two copies of the *Enquirer*. He examined the most recent of the two.

"I wonder," he ruminated slowly. "Would he seek out the Vanderkloot woman? It might be worth monitoring."

He reached for one of the blue telephones on the desk and made a quick call, issuing low, careful orders.

After he hung up, the intercom buzzed.

"Yes, Mrs. Mikulka?" he purred.

"It's Dr. Dooley. I'm afraid there's been a relapse. He said you'd want to know immediately."

"Ah, thank you. I will be down directly, Mrs. Mikulka."

"Yes, Mr. Ransome."

18

Waking up was the hardest part of Naomi Vanderkloot's day.

It was a life that had, since she'd joined the faculty of the University of Massachusetts, fallen into a rhythmic monotony of teaching two semesters with a break in January and the summer months off. She was a shoo-in for tenure, which would guarantee her frequent sabbaticals. Her salary was good, her Cambridge apartment was rent-controlled, yet in spite of her best efforts, she spent more time out of relationships than in them.

Hence the tragedy of waking up to an undemanding life and an always empty pillow beside her own.

Namoi Vanderkloot roused out of sleep reluctantly. She buried her face in the Crate and Barrel pillow to keep out the sunlight coming through the fern-choked window. One long-toed foot peeped out from under the cover to touch the polished hardwood floor beside her imported Japanese futon.

She didn't hear the footsteps in the long hallway outside her bedroom, nor the faint grinding of metal against paint as her bedroom door hinges swung. A crocheted throw rug wrinkled under silent footsteps and the hand that reached for her throat was careful to avoid the stray tendrils of her long hair until she felt them dig into her windpipe . . . and by then it was too late.

"Don't move," a hard male voice hissed.

"Mumpph."

"Not a word. I won't hurt you." The voice was as splintery as bamboo. Naomi felt her heart beating. She opened her eyes, but saw only pillow.

The hand was joined by another hand. This one pulled her head back by her straight hair to expose her face. Then it shifted to her mouth before she could scream.

When Naomi Vanderkloot's eyes flew open and she saw the upside-down face hovering over her, she no longer wanted to scream. She wanted to ask his name.

"Mumph!" she repeated.

"You know me?" the man asked. Naomi nodded briskly. He had those same drill-bit eyes, the high cheekbones and cruel mouth. His shoulders were not as broad as she would have liked, but shoulders weren't everything.

"Are you Professor Naomi Vanderkloot?" he demanded.

Naomi's nod was eager this time. She batted her eyes.

"Listen up, then. I'm going to let go of your mouth, but I'll still have my other hand on your throat. Understand?"

Naomi almost dislodged both hands with the enthusiasm of her nodding. The hand withdrew.

"It really *is* you!" she breathed, sitting up. "I can't believe it. I've dreamed of this moment. This is incredible. You have no idea what this means to— Mummph." The hand returned. This time it pinched her lips shut. Her tongue, caught between them, touched his fingertips. They tasted like oranges. smelled like them too.

"Stop drooling," he was saying. "I'm not here for your benefit. But for mine. Short answers, okay? And spare me the girlish enthusiasm. I'm having a bad week."

Naomi nodded demurely, her eyes drinking in her captor's strong white teeth. He possessed ordinary human canines, which surprised her. She had expected the next evolution to produce herbivores with small blunted teeth adapted for grinding salads, not tearing meat.

The hand withdrew tentatively, hovering over her face. The fingers were long, but blunt at the tips. Usually a sign of a slow sugar burner. She frowned.

"Now, do you know who I am?" he asked intently.

"Yes," she said, hoping that was short enough for him—not that she would mind his strong masculine hands back on her body.

"My name is Remo Williams. Does that name mean anything to you?"

"No. I mean, yes! The letters—some of them—said your first name was Remo."

"Letters?"

"From the *Enquirer* readers. I thought they were ridiculously unscientific, until so many of them came in saying your name was Remo. Most of them described the old Mongoloid to a T."

"Mongol? How do you know he's Mongol?"

"A Mongoloid, not a Mongolian," Naomi lectured. "A Mongoloid is simply an Asian. From certain genotypical clues—primarily the bone structure of the face and the Mongoloid eye fold—I've tentatively classified him as a member of the Altaic family, which includes the Turkish, Mongolian, and Tungusic peoples. I'm leaning toward Tungusic, which would make him Korean. Although he *could* be Japanese. Historically, there's been a lot of racial intermingling between those groups. The Japanese aren't part of the Tungusic family, of course, but—"

The hand started to move in again, and Naomi shut up like a constipated clam.

"I want to see these letters," Remo said.

"They're in the den. I can show you. If you'll let me up."

Both hands then withdrew, and Naomi composed her nightgown before getting up. She pulled on her owlish glasses.

"Hi!" she said, batting her eyes at his unresponsive face. He was nearly six feet tall. Probably of Mediterranean stock. His eyes were deeper than the descriptions. Like shark's eyes. They were merciless. They made Naomi shiver deliciously.

"Lead the way," he ordered.

Naomi started for the door, but her bare feet encountered the throw rug. It slid on the slick floor, upsetting her. She experienced an instant of flung-limbed imbalance. Her knees clicked together, her feet bending sideways at the ankles. She blinked, wondering why she wasn't falling.

Then Naomi noticed the steel-hard pressure at the back of her neck, which raised her to her feet.

"Oh, you caught me," she gasped as Remo released her from his one-handed grasp. "Great reflexes. You must burn your sugar really, really fast."

"What are you talking about?" Remo demanded peevishly.

"I'll explain later. Come on. I'll show you my files. They're much more interesting than those semiliterate letters."

"If you say so."

"Can I ask you some questions?" Naomi asked as they walked down the hall.

"No."

"Who were your parents?"

"No idea. I'm an orphan."

"Really?"

"I don't remember it being all that special," he growled.

"But you could come from anywhere. I don't detect an accent."

"I was raised in Newark, New Jersey. By nuns."

Naomi made a sympathetic face. "How terrible for you."

Remo shrugged. "It wasn't so bad."

They came to the den, where concrete-block-and-plywood bookshelves held scores of volumes. A copper filing cabinet stood beside a small desk.

"Top drawer. Under H," Naomi said helpfully.

"H for what?"

"*Homo crassi carpi.* That's the species name for you. I devised it myself. It's Latin for 'man the thick-wristed.' Do you like it?"

"Not really. But it beats 'Dead Man.' "

"That was that horrid *Enquirer* person's idea. He was hopelessly ethnocentric."

"Sit and be quiet."

Naomi sat. "Where are you from?" she asked. "I mean, after Newark. My files show no clear subsistence patterns. No territorial locus."

Remo pulled out a thick file and began leafing through closely typed pages. There were many typos.

"While you're just standing here doing nothing, can I measure your cephalic index?" Naomi asked hopefully.

"What?" Remo asked without looking up.

"It will take only a second. I have a tape measure on my desk." Naomi plucked a cloth measure in her fingers and stood up. She started to loop it around Remo's forehead, but one hand came up absently and snapped it without conscious effort.

"Wow! You really *do* burn your sugar," she said, blinking at the two dangling lengths of calibrated cloth. "I didn't even see your hand move."

"Sit down."

Naomi sat. "Mind if I take notes?" she asked meekly.

"Just do it quietly."

Naomi began writing on a notepad. Obviously a hominid, she noted. Good posture and bipedal locomotion. Cranial development normal for a twentieth-century male. It was odd. Except for the overdeveloped wrists, there were no outwardly distinctive divergences from genus *Homo sapiens*. Maybe if she could get him to take off his clothes . . .

Leaning closer, she got her first close look at those wrists. They were tremendously thick. A strange quality to possess. There were no muscles in the wrists to develop like that. Maybe it was a mutation. Yet the rest of him was so lean. Little body fat. He must eat very intelligently. Lots of salads.

"Tell me about your diet," Naomi prompted.

"Huh?"

"What was the last thing you ate?"

"Oranges. I stole them off a truck."

"A forager! I expected a hunter-gatherer because of your obviously nomadic migratory patterns. Do you eat meat?"

"I've been losing my taste for it."

"Just as I thought," Naomi said, scribbling on a notepad. "Excellent. Moving away from your bestial carnivore forebears. Isn't evolution grand?"

Remo looked up suddenly. "What are you babbling about?"

"I'm an anthropologist. I'm just trying to understand you."

"And I'm trying to understand these dippy reports. They have me—or someone who looks like me—running from hell and gone like a maniac. Destroying this. Breaking that."

"I've been trying to fathom your behavioral patterns. I came to the conclusion that you're trying to dismantle our stupid twentieth-century technolopolis. To pave the way for the reign of your own kind, am I right?"

"My kind?"

"*Homo crassi carpi.*"

"Lady, I don't swing that way. Not even after twenty years on the row."

"I said 'thick-wristed,' not 'limp-wristed.' And what do you mean by 'the row'? Is that the name of your kinship group? Do you belong to some kind of ceremonial clan?"

"That's what I can't figure," Remo muttered grimly. "If this is me in these reports, how could I have been in two places at once?"

Naomi blinked. "Now I don't understand *you*."

Remo shook the files under Naomi's narrow nose. "I've been on death row for the last twenty years," he snapped. "I haven't been outside prison walls since I broke jail last night."

"Jail? Those fascists!"

"What fascists?" Remo said, dumbfounded.

"The government. This is obviously a government plot. They learned of your existence—you, the next stage in human evolution—and they imprisoned you unjustly. Oh, you poor *Homo crassi carpi*."

"Government plot?"

"Yes, this fascist regime is committed to destroying anything it doesn't understand."

"Lady, I've been doing time for killing a pusher. I didn't do it, but that's why I was doing time."

"You were framed. It all fits."

"Read my lips. I said twenty years. I've been on death row for twenty years, not running around the country with a crazy old Mongol."

"Mongoloid. And who is he? I couldn't figure him out either."

"Damned if I know. But he's dead."

"Dead?"

"At least I think so. I saw him die in a dream. It seemed as real as those other dreams, the ones where I was doing stuff like you have in these files. But I don't remember being in any of these places or doing these things. Hell, before I was sent away, I'd barely ever been out of New Jersey. Unless you count a tour in Vietnam."

Naomi Vanderkloot touched Remo's arm tenderly.

"Don't try to sort it all out at once," she said. "You've been through a tremendous ordeal."

Remo slapped the files in her solicitous hands. "There's nothing in these to help me. Thanks for your time."

Naomi shot to her feet. Her eyes were pleading. "Wait! I can help you."

"Yeah, how? I'm in pretty deep."

"By offering you a place to stay for a start. Here. Then we'll help you find yourself. That's what this is all about, isn't it? Finding yourself."

"I know who I am. Remo Williams."

"And Remo Durock. And Remo DeFalco. And Remo Weeks. Don't you see? These reports can't all be coincidence. You may think you've been in jail, but someone with your face and first name has been doing all these bizarre destructive things."

"Maybe I have a twin brother," Remo suggested.

"Maybe. If so, then you and he are the same species. I want to study you. Please allow me."

Naomi Vanderkloot watched the changing expressions flicker across Remo Williams' troubled face. The doubt, the confusion, oh, he was everything she'd ever wanted in a man. Or a study specimen. He was perfect.

Seeing him waver, she reached up and removed her glasses. In movies, this was always the moment when the handsome hero fell for the brainy woman who, under the glasses and schoolmarm bun, was secretly gorgeous. And passionate. She wet her lips to communicate the passionate part. And waited for his reaction.

"Can you cook?" Remo asked at last.

Naomi's face fell. She struggled to get it aloft again.

"Yes," she said bravely.

"Good. I'm starving. Got any rice?"

"As much as you want. Plain white or wild?"

"Mix 'em."

"Let's continue this in the kitchen," Naomi suggested, smiling.

In the kitchen, Naomi asked, "Care for a Dove Bar while you wait?"

"I'll shower after we eat," Remo said seriously, watching in horrified fascination as Naomi Vanderkloot took a package from the freezer marked "Dove Bar" and began nibbling.

Later, over two heaping bowls of rice, she listened to Remo Williams' life story. It was not exactly a biography. More of a hard-luck story.

"And you say you simply woke up in Florida State Prison?" she asked when he was through. "And they said you'd killed a guard?"

"I *did* kill a guard," Remo said. "It took a while for it to come back to me, but I remember it distinctly. He pushed me to the breaking point. I guess I was treated like a criminal for so long, I became one."

Naomi placed a reassuring hand on Remo's massive wrist.

"Prison turns men into killers, even evolved men like you," she said simply. She squeezed and felt hard wrist bones.

"Why do you keep saying that? Men like me?"

"Because you're different. I've analyzed these reports. You're not like other men. You're a step ahead. I theorize that you're the leap ahead in human evolution. A mutant."

"Bulldookey. I was a beat cop who got jammed up in the justice system. End of story." He yanked free from her hands. He didn't like the creepy way she was feeling up his wrist.

"That doesn't explain how you escaped death row. How you manipulated electronic locks with your fingers."

Remo had no response to that. He chewed his

food slowly, carefully, before swallowing. Naomi wrote that down on the pad beside her plate and began to chew her food slowly for just as long as Remo. She waited until he swallowed before she did. By then, her rice had the consistency of liquid.

She wrote that down too.

"The way I figure it," she said at last, "we simply backtrack all the things you remember until we find a link."

"The name Folcroft Sanitarium seems to mean something. And a guy named Harry Smith. I thought he was the judge who sentenced me, but he seems connected to Folcroft somehow. If it exists."

"I think your dreams are tapping on the door of your subconscious. They're trying to tell you something. Yes, Folcroft would be an excellent place to start."

"But how would we find it? It could be anywhere."

"Just a moment," Naomi said, going to her telephone stand. She pulled out the white pages and brought the book to the table.

"What we'll do is call information for every area code in the country and ask if they have a listing for Folcroft. If it's out there, eventually we'll hit it."

Remo's eyebrows shot up in surprise. "Smart," he said.

"Thank you," Naomi said, pleased. "We'll start with New Jersey, because that's where you think you lived."

"That's where I *did* live," Remo said firmly.

"You think."

Remo frowned as Naomi went to the telephone.

There was no Folcroft Sanitarium in New Jersey, according to the information operator. Naomi then dialed New York State.

"I got it!" she cried, clapping her hand over the receiver. "It's in Rye, New York. Write this number down."

Remo wrote the numbers Naomi called out, wondering what this stuff on the pad about chewing food to a liquid was all about.

Naomi accepted the pad from Remo and dialed Folcroft Sanitarium. "Yes, hello. Could you connect me with Harry Smith?" Pause. "Oh, I see. No, I'm not a relative. The new director? What is his name, please? . . . I see. . . . No, that won't be necessary. Thank you."

Naomi hung up and turned to Remo with a triumphant smile, making her face resemble a hungry clown mask.

"What'd you learn?" Remo asked anxiously.

"We're onto something. There is *a* Harold Smith there. But he's a patient. They asked if I was a relative."

Remo's hopeful expression deflated. "Coincidence."

"Could be," Naomi said thoughtfully. "But you know, after I told them I wasn't a relative, they asked if I wanted to talk to the new director. That might mean Smith is the old director."

"Strange. Harold Smith was the judge who put me away. I remember it as plain as day."

"Maybe he switched careers?" Naomi suggested.

"Maybe. What was the new director's name?"

"Norvell Ransome. Does it ring a bell?"

"No. Never heard of the guy. I guess we're at a dead end."

"Let's leave that line of investigation for the moment. It'll keep." Naomi began dialing again.

"Who're you calling now?" Remo wanted to know.

"New Jersey information. Hello? . . . Yes, could I have the number of Trenton State Prison?" Naomi looked over at Remo. What could it hurt? her expression said.

19

Dr. Alan Dooley was nervously hovering around his patient when Norvell Ransome waddled into the green hospital room on the third floor of Folcroft Sanitarium. He did not look up as Ransome's prodigious shadow fell over the patient's corpse-gray face. Smith lay under an oxygen tent, intravenous tubes taped to one dead-looking arm.

"He's taken a turn for the worse, but I have him stabilized," Dooley said flatly.

"That is most unfortunate," Ransome said unctuously.

"What?" Dooley asked querulously. "That Smith's condition has worsened or that he's stabilized?"

"I resent that uncalled-for remark, sir," Ransome said, bending over the death mask of a face that belonged to Dr. Harold W. Smith. "You are forgetting your place."

"Sorry," Dr. Dooley said quietly.

"Perhaps your heart is no longer in your work. Hmmm?"

"You have my loyalty, and you know it."

"I have your genitals in my vise grips, Doctor. That is not loyalty. That is servitude, but it suits me and it befits you."

"You cold bastard," Dooley snapped. "I'd love to know where you learned about my . . . indiscretion."

"A fondness for prepubescent girls is not an indiscretion, sir. It is a disease. As for my sources, let us

153

say that I have access to a great many secrets. Your slimy little foibles being among the least of them. Now, update me on Dr. Smith's condition."

Dr. Dooley wiped his perspiring forehead. "He's still in a coma. His heart began fibrillating, but it stabilized by itself."

"He appears even more corpselike of visage than before, eh?"

"Illusion. When you haven't been here for a few days, it just seems that way because he's nearly the color of lead. We call the condition cynanosis. In Smith's case, the gray coloration is due to a congenital heart defect. There's a flaw in the wall of his left ventricle. I examined his medical records. Smith was a blue baby. The condition—which was the result of insufficient oxygenation of the blood—cleared up when he was still an infant, although the root cause obviously did not. Over the years, his heart has become enlarged. His wife tells me that his skin color had gradually darkened over the years. The shock that stopped his heart simply made the leadenness that much more pronounced."

"I see. And what, if anything, can you do for him?"

"It's touch and go. I'll continue to monitor him around the clock. If he relapses further, naturally I'll resuscitate."

"Hmmm," Norvell Ransome said softly. "I would prefer that you do not do that."

Dr. Dooley shot the fat man a glaring glance.

"I can't do that," he said heatedly. "You know that. No matter what you threaten me with."

Sizing up the fire in the physician's eyes, Norvell Ransome nodded. His pursy lower lip protruded like a hemorrhoid.

"I can see that, Doctor. Very well. Let me relieve you for a few days. You've obviously been under great strain."

"Not until you bring in another doctor," Dr. Dooley said firmly.

"I assure you that the Folcroft medical staff will be equal to the task. No, please. You have my word. Or would you prefer that I report your 'indiscretions' to the AMA?"

"You've made your point," Dr. Dooley said grudgingly.

His shoulders drooping, Dr. Dooley trudged from the hospital room. After he had departed, Norvell Ransome rummaged through a cabinet and found an ordinary box of Band-Aids. He selected a broad one and carefully peeled the backing as he walked over to Dr. Smith's still form. Smith's bluish lips were parted slightly, revealing dull dry teeth. His folded hands showed blued fingernails.

Reaching under the oxygen tent, Ransome affixed the Band-Aid across the patient's slate-gray forehead. The contrast with the flesh-colored Band-Aid was ghoulish. Then, extracting a fountain pen with a solid gold nub, he began to write on the Band-aid in a looping florid script, holding Smith's head still as he did so.

When he was done, he stepped back and read the result: DO NOT RESUSCITATE.

Noticing that he had forgotten to dot the I in "resuscitate," Ransome placed a precise dot in the proper place and, capping the pen, left the room.

To the floor nurse, he said, "Dr. Dooley will be taking a few days off. Please see that Dr. Smith is attended to by our top physician, won't you?"

"Yes, Mr. Ransome." She hurried off to do her duty.

Norvell Ransome allowed himself to admire the play of the nurse's womanly buttocks under the starched white uniform before waddling toward the elevator. He liked the way she had hurried to do his bidding. Like the governor of Florida. And unlike Dr. Dooley.

Soon, many would do his bidding. Not tomorrow, or next month, perhaps. Great plans took time to germinate. Ransome stabbed the down button, and happily, the elevator responded instantly.

He stepped aboard and pressed two. The cage sank and Norvell Ransome felt the thrill of momentary weightlessness in his 334-pound being.

It had been an interesting week. Only seven days ago, Norvell Ransome had been a GG-18 with the National Security Agency, the Department of Defense's critical communications security arm, working in its Fort Meade computer section, when he was summoned to the office of the NSA director, known in the agency's parlance as DIRNSA.

Ransome took the elevator that day too, enjoying the buoyancy of the ride. He loved elevators, and the effect they had on his normally ponderous body.

The blue-uniformed Federal Protective Service guard that day had checked the laminated plastic photo I.D. card dangling under Ransome's three-ply chin and allowed him to waddle unmolested down Mahogany Row, the ninth-floor executive offices, to the bright blue door at the corridor's end, emblazoned with the NSA seal, an eagle clutching a skeleton key.

Ransome entered Room 9A197, checked in with the executive secretary, and was instantly buzzed into the director's comfortable but businesslike office.

The director waved Ransome to a leather armchair, then, catching himself, said, "The couch, if you prefer."

"Thank you sir," Ransome said unself-conciously. The armchair had looked substantial, but Ransome had been known to burst the rear tires on a taxi simply by climbing into the back seat.

"I am holding up a file," the director said crisply. "Do you see the code on front?"

"TOP SECRET CURE," Ransome said, frowning. He

was familiar with most NSA codes. Top Secret Umbra, for example. Or the Gamma class—Gyro, Gilt, Gout, etc.—which was reserved for matters pertaining to Soviet intelligence.

"This is so you recognize it when it arrives at your home by Federal Express tomorrow morning."

Ransome blinked. "Why not simply hand it to me?"

"Too risky. I can't have every FPS officer from here to the Cyclone fence trying to trace it back to its source. Officially this file does not exist. Officially we never had this meeting. Is that understood?"

"Yes, sir." But of course Norvell Ransome had not understood.

"I doubt that," DIRNSA said. "I don't understand any of this myself. This was messengered over here from the White House. I was told if I opened the file, it would be my neck."

"Who would threaten you, sir?"

"The President of the United States," the director said flatly. "And I may be known as a wheels-up ballsy SOB, but the President is ex-CIA. As much as it galls me to do so, this time I'm just following orders. Tomorrow morning at ten-thirty, Federal Express will deliver this to your door. Sign for it. Study it. Then destroy it. As soon as you have done so, you will go directly to the airport and board a plane for whatever destination is indicated in this file. You will remain on station indefinitely, unless you are relieved. Until such time, consider yourself on leave from all NSA duties."

"On leave? Where?"

"I do not know. And you will not tell me. We will never discuss this matter once you leave my office. The President personally asked me to assign this matter to my most trustworthy computer engineer."

"Thank you, sir."

"Don't thank me. This whole thing reeks of plausible deniability. There's a good reason for the President not to assign this to the CIA, and I don't want to think what that reason might be."

Norvell Ransome swallowed uncomfortably. He realized immediately that he could be an expendable component in a larger operation. He did not enjoy contemplating that notion.

"Do I have the option to decline this assignment?" he asked.

"I frankly do not know. But if this is as critical as it sounds, I'd say you already know too much to turn it down."

"I believe I shall accept, then," Ransome had said quickly.

"Wise career move."

Norvell Ransome pushed himself to his tiny feet. It took three tries before he successfully levered himself up into a bandy-legged standing stance. ·

He walked away trembling from head to toe. The director hadn't even bothered to say good-bye.

The Federal Express package arrived at exactly 10:28 A.M. the next day. Ransome signed for it and pulled open the envelope flap. Inside was the folder stamped TOP SECRET CURE. Before leaving the office the day before, he had run down every code name in the NSA data base. CURE was not one of them. He wondered what it could mean, but there was no point in pondering the matter. DOD code names never reflected their actual meaning or subject matter.

Inside the file was a description of an electronic listening post set up in a private facility known as Folcroft Sanitarium in Rye, New York. There was a brief description of its computer system and passwords. Nothing about its mission.

A simple note on presidential stationery said: "Continue operations until notified." It was not signed.

Norvell Ransome arrived at Folcroft by airport

limousine less than five hours later. He was met by a flustered secretary, a Mrs. Mikulka, who handed him a sealed envelope and told him Dr. Smith's condition had not changed.

Ransome had wondered who Dr. Smith was as he was led to the second-floor office marked "Harold W. Smith, Director." He opened the envelope in the privacy of the man's office. The desk chair was sturdy. It would support his weight, he thought as he read through the letter signed by Smith.

The letter left out more than it revealed. It told of a hidden stud under the lip of the desk. Ransome found and depressed it. A computer terminal suddenly rose from a concealed well on his left.

With the skill of a professional programmer, Ransome brought up the system and was met by a scrolling series of news and information digests. He had no idea where they were coming from. They were totally random facts. Word that an illegal hostile takeover was in progress against a defense-critical industry. A CIA burn notice warning of a Soviet mole in the U.S. State Department. Statistics, and what he finally deduced were NSA-style "gists" of telephone intercepts that conclusively showed that a high-level politician was arranging for a cocaine shipment to enter his city. The politician was not identified except by telephone number.

Ransome called the number and got the governor's mansion in Florida. He hung up without speaking.

Whatever Folcroft was, Norvell Ransome realized, its apparent mission was similar to the NSA message-traffic intelligence gathering. Here was electronic intelligence gathering at its finest. With a start, Ransome realized that some of this information was familiar. He had passed it through the dozen acres of computers—that was how they measured computer capacity at NSA, in acres—only yesterday.

"My God. This is being siphoned off our systems," he said hoarsely.

Not only NSA computers, it turned out, but CIA, FBI, DIA, IRS, Pentagon, and uncountable business and private sources.

The enormity of that realization was just sinking in when a muffled ringing interrupted. He picked up the blue standard telephone, but there was just a dial tone in his baby-shiny ear. The ringing continued. He looked around. There was no other phone. Ransome had reached out to buzz the secretary when he realized it was coming from the upper-right-hand desk drawer.

Ransome pulled out the drawer, and there, amid a profusion of aspirin and antacid bottles, was a bright red telephone with a flat blank area where the dial should have been. Puzzled, Ransome plucked up the receiver.

"Who am I speaking with, please?" a dry familiar voice asked. The accent was a jumble of clipped New England consonants and Texas twang.

"Norvell Ransome."

"This is your President, Mr. Ransome. Are you up and running?"

"Indeed I am, Mr. President."

"Please enter the password RESTORE. Shall I spell that?"

"No, I have it," Ransome had said, complying instantly. His fingers were shaky on the keys. The scrolling data extracts vanished. A cursor began spinning out blocks of text. He read along in silence, his eyes becoming white-edged eggs in his fleshy pear of a face.

"Are you prepared to execute the orders summarized?" the President had demanded.

"Yes, sir."

"When you have succeeded, simply pick up the

receiver you are holding and so inform me. Otherwise, continue operations. Do you understand?"

"Yes."

"What is the latest on Dr. Smith?"

"The staff is worried about him," Ransome answered truthfully.

"Notify me of any changes in his prognosis. Good luck, Ransome." The click was soft but quite final.

Ransome replaced the receiver woodenly. This was a field operation, and not what he had entered the NSA for. True, his qualifications were admirably suited to the task of continuing ELINT monitoring, but this other thing . . .

Ransome read the instructions several times, until he had his nerve up, and then he began to input the commands that would set into motion the first phase of his first task as . . . He didn't know what he was, other than the new director of Folcroft.

Within twenty-four hours he had begun to get an inkling. He had discovered several levels of coded computer files within the Folcroft system which he could not enter. As a graduate in the NSA's National Cryptological School, he was presented with a challenge he could not resist. He moistened his bud lips and plunged in.

It turned out to be a challenge beyond his abilities, despite his having earned the National Security Medal and the Travis Trophy for cryptanalysis work. Not without help.

The director of the NSA had chosen wisely when he chose Norvell Ransome, graduate of Princeton and expert code breaker. He was perfect for this job. He was also, unfortunately, a man driven to solve problems and dismantle mysteries by virtue of an uncontrollable curiosity. The very impenetrability of the Folcroft complex was simply too great to ignore. He dialed a number that tied the Folcroft system into the NSA mainframes and commanded the agency's batteries of supercomputers to attack the Folcroft code. He chose the so-called "brute-force" method, whereby virtually every unoccupied NSA computer attempted possible solutions at a rate of thousands of cycles per second.

No code, no matter how elegant, could resist such a decrypting assault for very long, he knew. The Folcroft computers resisted for an astounding seventy-two hours, but finally, at 5:33 on a Thursday afternoon, it was all there for Norvell Ransome to digest.

Folcroft was the cover for a supersecret U.S. government agency called CURE. It was brilliant, Ransome thought. The code name was actually the agency name. Had he made the connection independently, he would have dismissed it as simple coincidence.

According to the files, CURE had been set up in the early 1960's by a now-deceased president. The country was tearing itself apart. Social anarchy lay ahead. Declaring permanent martial law and repealing the Constitution seemed the only option. But the young President had found a third alternative. So CURE was created. At first run by an ex-CIA bureaucrat named Harold W. Smith, it was an information clearinghouse for criminal activity. Working off and through ordinary law-enforcement agencies, Smith had orchestrated counterforce assaults against the growing criminal element, thereby keeping America from plunging into the abyss. But it was not enough.

After several years, a new president decided that CURE would need an enforcement arm. One man was selected. An ordinary man who would be trained in an obscure martial art that Ransome had never even heard of. One man. A police officer named Remo Williams, whom the world had long believed dead thanks to a CURE-engineered murder frame-up and a rigged execution. The man whom Ransome had gotten out of the way through Project RESTORE, he realized. It made sense. Still, one man?

That puzzle could be solved later. It was the operational details of CURE that intrigued Ransome. The President did not control CURE, although he could order it disbanded. There was no oversight. Its annual budget was enormous, yet it was so secret, it never appeared in congressional budgets. It was not black-budget, like NSA and certain defense programs. It was totally off-the-books. It simply didn't exist. None of it existed.

Yet somehow, for nearly thirty years, it had functioned in secret, holding the nation together—until the day its director, Dr. Harold W. Smith, had had a heart attack while shopping.

It was this accident, unexpected but foreseen, as were a number of other emergency contingencies, that had forced the President to turn to the NSA, and the DIRNSA to turn to Norvell Ransome.

It all made sense. Ransome would run CURE until Smith recovered. Or, failing that, until the President chose to replace Smith or, more conceivably, shut down CURE altogether.

Seated in Dr. Smith's cracked leather chair, the deepest, ugliest secrets of the nation washing his face in phosphorescent green, Norvell Ransome vowed to himself that he would become the next director of CURE, no matter what it took.

All he had to do was eliminate Smith and the enforcement arm. And fortunately, Smith himself had provided an elegant solution to the latter problem.

Now, a week later, the Remo Williams matter had resurfaced. Dr. Smith would take care of it himself. The man was never going to recover. But Williams' escape was untidy.

Returning to his office, Ransome walked past Mrs. Mikulka and whispered softly, "It does not look good."

Whereupon Mrs. Mikulka reached for a handker-
chief and buried her face in it.

Dr. Smith's chair groaned under Ransome's set-
tling weight. He briefly glanced at the ELINT data
on the terminal screen. There was an alert light
flashing. Frowning, Ransome tapped a key.

Electronic transcripts popped onto the screen. There
had been another call made to Trenton State Prison
inquiring about a former prisoner named Remo Williams. Ransome had programmed the computer's
telephone-traffic intercepts to key-off Williams' name.
Warden McSorley's call had been a potential problem, but had settled itself. But who was this new
person? Ransome lined up the cursor with the iden-
tifying telephone number and hit a key.

He was annoyed, but not surprised, to read that it
belonged to Professor Naomi Vanderkloot, the anthropologist who had broken the Remo Williams story
to, of all places, the *National Enquirer*. It was,
Ransome had determined through backtracking, the
probable incident that had triggered Dr. Smith's heart
failure. When he had learned of that, Ransome had
elected to allow the matter to run its natural course.
Who read the *Enquirer*? Certainly no one who could
possibly be a player on the national stage.

Unfortunately, that had been a mistake, for through
a fluke, Remo Williams had seen a copy.

This confirmed Ransome's suspicion that Williams
would make contact with the Vanderkloot woman. A
cross-reference light blinked. There was an earlier
telephone intercept, Ransome found. This one was
even more troubling. The same Naomi Vanderkloot
had called Folcroft to inquire about Dr. Smith. How
could she have known about Folcroft? Not from Williams. Williams knew only what Project RESTORE
allowed him to remember. Williams' trainer, the
Korean known as Chiun, was in Korea, oblivious of
the events of the past week. And Smith was comatose.

* * *

Norvell Ransome steepled his blunt fingers. His eyebrows drew together like furry caterpillars kissing. This was unforeseen. And unfortunate. He must think this through. He had handled Project RESTORE expertly, as if he were born to such tasks. He would handle this with equal aplomb. He must not rush into a rash action. He knew where Remo was. Perhaps there was a way to lure him back to Folcroft, where he could be attended to.

There was no rush. First, it would be necessary to allow Dr. Smith to pass from this world of natural causes. The President of the United States would no doubt recognize the exemplary job Norvell Ransome was doing and ask him to stay on as director of Folcroft Sanitarium and the secret installation it concealed. During that time, he would quietly groom the governor of Florida for the White House. He was excellent presidential timber. Provided his cocaine-trafficking activities remained solely a CURE secret.

Then and only then would America become the vassal of Norvell Ransome.

Remo Williams would be just a bump on that exceedingly smooth road.

Ransome hunched over the CURE computer. It would all fall into place in time. But first there was the ultimate secret of Folcroft to uncover. What did the acronym CURE stand for? It was a nagging piece of intelligence not found in any of the files. Perhaps there were deeper levels to plumb. If so, Norvell Ransome would descend into them. The meaning of CURE might not be germane to its future, but Norvell Ransome was determined to fathom it.

20

Remo Williams paced the floor as Naomi Vanderkloot sat at the kitchen table, her back to him, the telephone to her ear.

"Anything?" he snapped.

"I'm still on hold. Why don't you just sit down?"

"This is driving me crazy," Remo said. His hands, hanging idle from his thick wrists, brushed his dungaree pockets. He felt the bulge there, and remembered the pack of Camels.

Remo pulled them out. They were mangled, but smokable. He fished one out and took the dry paper between his lips. Forgetting that matches were no longer precious, he turned on the gas stove and bent down to light the cigarette.

Almost immediately, he felt himself gag.

Naomi turned.

"You're smoking!" she cried, aghast.

"I'm nervous. Okay?"

"Smoking. I can't believe it. It's so . . . so third-world. Almost no one smokes these days."

"Well, I do," Remo said rackingly, wondering what was wrong with him that he couldn't smoke a simple unfiltered cigarette.

"What's that?" Naomi said into the phone as she batted bluish smoke away from her face. "Yes, I'm still here. . . . Where? . . . Are you certain? . . . Yes, thank you." She hung up and turned to Remo.

"I just spoke with the caretaker of a place called Wildwood Cemetery in New Jersey. He sounded a hundred years old. He confirms what the Trenton administration official told me. A convict named Remo Williams was buried there after his execution by electrocution."

"Then he was right," Remo said, sick-eyed.

"Who?"

"The Florida executioner. He said he already did me. How can I be here if I'm buried in New Jersey?"

"Look. You're not dead. That's obvious. You're the victim of some kind of . . . plot, I don't know. This sounds exactly like the kind of thing the CIA would do."

Remo leaned against the kitchen wall, running one hand through his hair. The cigarette smoldered in his other hand unnoticed. Annoyed, Naomi waved the smoke away with swipes of her hand.

"I dream dreams that seem more real than when I'm awake," Remo said in a baffled monotone. "My head feels heavy. I can't think straight. What the hell happened to me?"

Naomi came to her feet and approached him, her face suddenly tender.

"Look, don't try to sort it all out at once. You're here. You're with me. And you're safe. I'll help you sort the pieces. Just, let's take our time. I have more questions."

"Okay, okay," Remo said irritably, allowing himself to be led into the living room and onto the couch. He frowned when he noticed Naomi lift a pencil to her ever-present notepad.

"Let's start with your sex life," she began eagerly.

"What sex life?" Remo growled. "I've been on death row so long I forgot where to put it."

Naomi wrote "Crude" on her notepad. Reading that, Remo folded his arms angrily.

"Before you went to jail, then," Naomi went on. "How did you do it?"

"What kind of question is that? I just did it."

"I'm only interested in the courship and precopulation rituals you relied upon."

"The what? Look, dingbat, get this through your head: I'm an ordinary guy. I don't do it any differently than anyone else. Better, maybe. Not different."

Naomi inscribed something unreadable on her notepad and asked, "I don't suppose you happen to know how long your penis is?"

"I never thought to measure it," Remo said acidly. "Why?"

"As man developed from the primitive stage, his sex organs have enlarged and become more specialized. As the next stage in human development, it's important to know if there have been any further . . . specializations."

"Important to whom?" Remo asked sourly.

"Science," Naomi stuttered. "This is the pursuit of knowledge. If I can codify the traits that make you unique, we would be able to identify others on the vanguard of evolution, and if they can be persuaded to mate, a new, improved race would emerge generations earlier than otherwise."

"So?"

"So then we can study you and your kind."

"Lady, it wouldn't work that way. It would be the Europeans and the Indians all over again. Someone would win and someone would lose. Why push it along any faster? Let it be."

"You don't understand science."

"I don't want to. I'm trying to understand my life."

"Does that mean you won't let me measure your penis?"

"Good guess. I'm an escaped felon, remember?"

Naomi smiled. "I find that extra-exciting."

Remo rolled his eyes. "You would."

She leaned closer. "You interest me," she breathed, her mouth smelling of coffee yogurt.

"I'm a killer," Remo reminded her.

Naomi inched closer on the sofa. She tossed back her hair and lowered her face so that she had to give Remo an up-from-under look. She pushed her glasses up onto her forehead.

"You probably haven't had sex in twenty years," she said.

"I *definitely* haven't had sex for twenty years," Remo said.

"Well," Naomi Vanderkloot said with what she hoped was a sexy smile, "now's your golden opportunity."

Remo Williams' glance took in the foolish smile that came over Naomi Vanderkloot's thin face, went down to her flat chest, lingered on her whalebone hips, and decided beggars couldn't be choosers.

"You're on," he said, taking her by the hand. Remo led her to the bedroom, unaware that her other hand still clutched her notepad and pencil.

"What are you doing with that?" Remo asked moments later. Naomi Vanderkloot lay under him, her face flushed, one hand reaching down to his crotch. The hand clutched a pencil.

"Umm. Nothing," she said absently.

"You're holding a pencil against my tool," Remo pointed out in a reasonable voice. "I don't exactly call that nothing."

Naomi withdrew the pencil and used it to scribble a single-digit number onto the notepad by her pillow.

"Are you through?" Remo demanded. "Can we get on with this?"

"Absolutely." Naomi closed her eyes. Remo noticed she folded her hands over her stomach as if steeling herself for an ordeal. He entered her slowly, watching the play of expressions on her narrow face. They began with concern, softened to delight, and tightened up again as Remo fell into a slow, building rhythm.

Just when Remo was getting into it, Naomi's right eye peeked open. Remo stopped in mid-stroke.

"What are you looking at?" Remo wanted to know.

"I wanted to see if your body was flushed. It's a sexual response found only in the higher primates."

"And?"

"Looks normal."

"Hooray for higher primates," Remo muttered. "Can we resume now, or would you like to take my temperature?"

"I already know your temperature," Naomi said archly. "You're *hot*. Like me."

"Thank you." Remo started again. He was just getting his concentration back when suddenly Naomi's eyes flew open and her hands clutched his naked chest.

"Oh, my God. You've been in *prison!*"

Remo stopped. "Is that just dawning on you?"

"You could have AIDS. I forgot all about it."

"What's AIDS?" Remo asked seriously.

Naomi frowned. "Don't tell me you never heard of AIDS."

"Never."

"Get off."

"I was just getting started."

"Get off! We'll finish later," Naomi said in a brisk, businesslike voice. She gathered up her pad and pencil and assumed a seated position on the futon. With a disgusted look on his face, Remo did the same.

"AIDS is a sexually transmitted disease," Naomi said officiously. "It's the biggest news story of the last ten years. And you never heard of it."

"Never," Remo said solemnly. He raised his right hand for effect, hoping to get this over with quickly.

"What if I told you that Ronald Reagan was president?"

"I'd ask of what?"

"The United States of America," Naomi said flatly.

"When did that happen?"

"Ten years ago. He's out of office now."

"Can't be. I know who's president. It's . . ." Remo stopped.

"Never mind. Who is Pee-Wee Herman?"

"A baseball player?"

"What does the phrase 'Made in Japan' mean to you?"

"A joke."

"You *are* out of touch."

Remo felt his manhood shrink as the questions came on. Finally Naomi looked up from her pad.

"You say you've been on death row for twenty years, but you don't know some of the most basic facts of American social life that have occurred over that span of time."

"We don't get to read much on death row," Remo said defensively.

"How much do you remember of your time at Trenton?"

"Stuff. Different people. It all kinda runs together. You live in the same cell most of the time. What's to remember, except the walls?"

"Tell me every concrete memory you can dredge up," Naomi prompted.

Remo sighed. His responses were slow, halting.

When he was through, Naomi looked at the fragmentary answers inscribed in her notepad.

"Your memory has been tampered with," she said firmly. "You have some kind of weird amnesia. I'm no psychologist, but you seem to have memories of things that may never have happened, yet at the same time, you don't remember things that you obviously were doing."

"How can that be?"

"I don't know," Naomi Vanderkloot said, looking

down at Remo's lap with one eye closed and her thumb and forefinger poised like a pincer.

Remo looked down at himself. "What are you doing?"

"Measuring it. It's called Anthropometry."

"You already did that."

"That was tumescent. This is flaccid."

"This is crap," Remo said, getting to his feet. He drew on his black guard's pants and T-shirt.

"Wait! Where are you going?" Naomi cried.

"To Folcroft. I'm not getting diddly here."

21

For the Master of Sinanju, the long journey ended at the closed gates of what was known in the scrolls he maintained as Fortress Folcroft, wrongly believed by some to be a lunatic asylum.

The taxi stopped at the gate under the brooding faces of the stone lion heads that looked down from the wrought-iron gate.

"Why do you stop here?" Chiun, Reigning Master of Sinanju, demanded querulously.

"The freaking guards won't open the gate," the cabby complained.

Chiun lowered his head to see beyond the driver's witless head. He saw that the wrought-iron portcullis was closed. Two guards stood beyond it, their weapons raised.

Chiun's wizened visage pinched up in surprise. These were true guards, not the feeble old men

Smith had formerly employed. Had some threat to his emperor reared up in his absence?

"I will speak with them," Chiun told the driver. "Remove my belongings from the trunk."

The Master of Sinanju stepped from the back and strode, his hands tucked into the sleeves of his saffron kimono, to the locked gates.

"I am Chiun," he said sternly to the hard-faced guards. But within his heart he was pleased. Smith had obviously doubled the guards during his absence. It was a tribute to his emperor's regard for the services of the Master of Sinanju.

"Are you a patient?" one the the guards asked.

Chiun drew himself up haughtily. "I serve Harold Smith."

The other guard looked at the one who had asked the impertinent question. They nodded in unison, gazes locked.

Chiun allowed a pleased smile to overtake his wrinkled face. They understood.

The gates opened automatically. It was another new security innovation, another tribute to the esteem in which America held Sinanju.

Chiun turned to the taxi driver, who was heaving his luggage from the taxi trunk with huffing sounds.

"Have a care with my property, white," he warned.

Then he felt an unmistakable preattack warning. He turned in a swirl of kimono skirts to behold the unbelievable sight of the two guards bearing down on him with hostile intent.

Chiun allowed them to feel the fineness of his kimono for a brief space of time as they attempted— and this was the truly unbelievable part—to take him in their naked, weaponless hands.

"There now—" one of them started to say.

And then he fell silent as he tried to clutch his own offending hand. The other guard's eyes went wide. Pain signals must have become confused in the

first guard's tiny brain, for he attempted to grasp his
uninjured hand with the other, not realizing—until
he lifted to his shocked face the erupting red stump
it had become—that he no longer had fingers with
which to grasp.

Both guards stumbled off in silent fright. Chiun
turned to the driver, who had witnessed none of
this.

"Return my luggage to your vehicle," he commanded.

"What? You change your mind?"

"No. The guards did. They have graciously con-
sented to allow your vehicle to enter these walls."

Unhappily, the driver restored Chiun's steamer
trunks and got behind the wheel. He drove through
the gates, unaware that the splintering sounds under
his wheel were not branches, but finger bones.

Seated in back, Chiun decided that the guards
were not a token of esteem after all. The physical
presence of the Master of Sinanju was not necessary
to deter enemies. Merely the knowledge that Sinanju
stood by a kingdom was enough. Chiun would so
inform Smith—after he scolded him for the rudeness
of his new and unnecessary guards.

The lobby-reception-desk person was also new.
He declined to allow the Master of Sinanju to see
Dr. Smith.

"Dr. Smith isn't allowed visitors," he said firmly.
"Unless you are family, which I can see you are not."

"What! Smith denies me!" Chiun flared. "I, who
have been like a father to him." The Master of Sinanju
waited for the functionary's reaction. It was a white
expression he had heard used to good effect on day-
time television dramas in the days when they were
worthy of his attention.

"You can't be serious," the functionary said.

The Master of Sinanju had heard that expression
on TV as well. It was usually followed by the laughter of unseen people—the same ones who laughed at

every bad joke yet sat silent during the truly humorous portions of certain offensive programs called sitcoms.

Chiun decided that this person was unimportant and glided past him to the elevators. The functionary called out the word "Guard!" once and Chiun listened to the yelling of the converging guards as the elevator door closed on his stern visage. Something was amiss at Fortress Folcroft. Smith had much explaining to do.

Emerging on the second floor, Chiun was pleased to see the same woman holding forth at Smith's reception desk. She was known as Smith's secretary, an odd designation, Chiun thought, for she knew none of Smith's secrets.

"Hail, servant of Smith. Please inform him of my arrival."

"I . . . that is . . . you haven't heard. I mean—"

"Why do you babble so, woman? Do this!"

"One moment." She stabbed at an intercom button and said, "There is a . . . person here who is asking about Dr. Smith. I believe he's a former patient."

"Yes, I have been expecting him. Allow him to enter, Mrs. Mikulka."

Chiun's parchment wrinkles scattered at the sound of the unfamiliar voice. Before the woman could rise from her seat, he hurried to the door and closed it behind him so rapidly it seemed to Mrs. Mikukla he melted through the unopened panel.

"I am Chiun, Master of Sinanju," Chiun announced in a cold voice. "And if you do not present to me a certain document, I will lay your entrails at your very feet."

The fat man sitting behind Dr. Smith's desk lost his composed expression. Tiny globules—that was the only word for them—of sweat erupted from his corrugated brow.

"Yes. Of course. I have it right here," he said quickly.

The Master of Sinanju accepted the proffered document. His hazel eyes glanced over it; then he returned to the fat man.

"What has become of Smith?" he asked, stiff-voiced.

"I am Norvell Ransome. I am the new director of Folcroft."

"And I do not care. Where is Smith?"

"Dr. Smith is ill. I have taken his place by presidential directive, as that letter implies. I was informed by the *Harlequin*'s captain that you had returned to America prematurely. May I inquire why?"

"No, you may not. I will see Smith."

"That is quite impossible right now. As your superior, I must ask you—"

"You are my superior only in body fat, gross one," Chiun snapped.

"I beg your pardon!" Norvell Ransome exploded. Indignation sent spittle spewing out of his round mouth.

"I do not serve you. Only Smith. No Master of Sinanju is permitted to serve a succeeding emperor, lest it be thought that Sinanju arranged the downfall of the first emperor. Now, I ask again: Where is Smith?"

"I promise you that you will see him shortly. And I have not succeeded Smith, as you so quaintly put it. I am merely replacing him until he is well. I believe that gets around your ancestral injunction against succeeding, er, emperors, does it not?"

"One does not get around correct thinking," Chiun sniffed. "One follows it. Now, Smith."

"As you please," Ransome said nervously. "Come with me."

The Master of Sinanju followed the corpulent man to the elevator, up to the third floor, and to a hospital-room door.

"Please wait here while I see if Smith is presentable."

"Be warned, I will not wait long."

"I'll only be a moment." And true to his word, Ransome returned shortly to open the door for the Master of Sinanju. The man's body reeked. Every pore exuded mingled food odors that each movement renewed.

Chiun drifted to the bedside of his emperor. At a glance, he could see that Smith was dying. The deathliness of the skin. The ragged breathing.

"The doctors say his prognosis is quite good," Ransome purred.

"The doctors are wrong," Chiun snapped. "He is failing."

"Oh, dear. I sincerely hope not." Ransome's voice was plaintive. "I have a very important assignment for you, which must be undertaken immediately."

"I will honor my contract," Chiun said simply. Ransome's jowly face perked up. "While Smith lives," he added.

Ransome's face sagged like taffy under a heat lamp.

"I wish a few moments with Smith," Chiun said.

"Why?"

"Respect. A word you should commit to memory."

"I shall be outside," Ransome said aridly.

After the man had gone, Chiun lifted the oxygen tent and felt Smith's neck artery. The pulse was thready. He noticed the shower cap over Smith's sparse hair and wondered if a brain operation—a barbarism whites practiced because they lacked knowledge of the correct herbs—had been performed on Smith. Pushing the plastic back, Chiun saw no marks of bone saw or suture. Only a plastic bandage on the forehead with the words DO NOT RESUSCITATE inscribed in ink.

The Master of Sinanju removed the Band-Aid before he replaced the shower cap. He laid a bony hand over Smith's heart. Its muscles beat very close

to the ribs. Enlarged. There was a gurgle in each
beat, indicating damaged chambers.

Chiun laid both hands over Smith's heart. He
closed his eyes, moving his fingers exploringly. When
he found a certain vibration, he struck. His fist lifted,
fell. Smith's body jumped. Chiun's eyes flew open.
He lifted one of Smith's eyelids. His expression registered disappointment.

He laid an ear to Smith's heart, and then, his face
sad, he replaced the oxygen tent. Solemnly Chiun
returned to the corridor.

"He is gravely ill," Chiun intoned.

"He is receiving the best of care, I assure you,"
Ransome said. "Now, shall we conclude our little
get-acquainted session in my office?"

Back in Smith's former office, the Master of Sinanju
stood in silence as Ransome pulled a copy of the
National Enquirer from a drawer. He displayed it so
that the likeness of Remo Williams faced the Master
of Sinanju.

"I believe you know what this means," he said.

"It means that Smith's mania for secrecy does not
sleep with him."

"No. The woman who's responsible for this out-
rage called Folcroft only hours ago, asking questions.
We don't know what she wants. Or how much she
knows about CURE. With Remo still on assignment,
you are my only resource."

"Remo's assignment. It is not going well?"

"There are some problems. I believe I explained
in my first message that Remo had gone undercover
in a prison."

"That message was from you?"

"Ah, yes. I signed it 'Smith' so you would not be
concerned."

"The second message was not signed at all," Chiun
pointed out.

"A lapse on my part."

"I see," Chiun said vaguely. "Tell me of this assignment of Remo's. It is very unusual?"

"It's too complicated to explain," Ransome assured him. "But I expect him to remain there at least another three weeks, gathering evidence."

"I understand," Chiun said softly. But he thought: What madness is this? Remo is not a compiler of evidence. Such duties are for file clerks and detectives. Remo's task to is eliminate enemies.

"Here," Ransome was saying as he transferred his gaze from his computer screen to a notepad. He wrote furiously and handed the top sheet to the Master of Sinanju.

"Her name is Naomi Vanderkloot. That is her address. Eliminate her. Today."

"Do you wish it to appear as an accident, or would something more public be preferred?"

Ransome's mouth became a red rosebud. "Public?"

"Yes. Something to warn your enemies that such will be their fate should they dare uncover your secrets."

"No. That would be counterproductive. But I don't mind if it's messy. In fact, why don't you make it look like a rape?"

Chiun stiffened. "A rape?"

"No, better," Ransome said, licking his pursy mouth. "Like she was gang-banged to death. Can you arrange that?"

"I will consider it," Chiun said distastefully.

"Excellent. By tonight. There's no telling what that woman is up to. I will make the arrangements for your travel. Please wait in the downstairs lobby."

"As you wish," the Master of Sinanju said, bowing formally. He noticed that the gesture went unheeded as Norvell Ransome picked up the telephone and began dialing.

Chiun withdrew. As he rode the elevator down, he looked again at the address on the sheet of paper

Ransome had given him. He was not reading the address. He had memorized it at first glance. He was comparing the loops and swoops of the handwriting with the notation on Smith's forehead. They were the same. Chiun placed the scrap of paper in a hidden pocket of his kimono as he stepped into the lobby.

The guards looked at him warily, and he ignored them, for he was deep in thought.

It was unfortunate. If Smith died, it would be the end of Chiun's work in America, richest of Sinanju clients. The man called Norvell Ransome was hardly worthy of Sinanju service, but in time he could be educated in kingly ways. He was, in some respects—both good and bad—very much like Nero the Good. Too bad. There were so few Neros in the modern world. . . .

22

"Please don't leave me, I beg of you," Naomi Vanderkloot wailed.

"Do you mind?" Remo Williams said impatiently. "I need that foot to walk with. Let go."

"Not until you promise to stay. I want you."

"I can tell. I can't remember the last time I had a woman get down on her knees like this. Don't you feel embarrassed—you, a professor?"

"No. It's my mating strategy. In primate courting behavior, the female withholds her favors until she finds a male primate with whom she's willing to mix gene pools. You're him. For me, I mean. Take my genes. They're yours."

"I don't want your genes," Remo said, bending down and prying her fingers off his ankle. They jumped to his calf. Remo rolled his eyes ceilingward. "I've heard of women who fall for cons, but I never thought it would happen to me."

"That's not it at all," Naomi protested, hurt.

"Look. If I stay, will you behave? No more notebooks or pencils?"

"I swear."

"Okay."

Naomi Vanderkloot jumped to her feet. Her face was a quarter-inch from Remo's. Her eyes were wide with appeal.

"Now?" she asked breathily. "I'm feeling very labial all of a sudden." That goofy smile came on again. Only this time it was more like a leer.

"Labial?" Remo said.

" 'Horny,' to you."

" 'Horny' I understand," Remo said. He was surprised at himself as they walked back to the bedroom. He was not looking forward to this at all. . . .

An hour later, it was growing dark. Remo was lying back on the pillow, smoking thoughtfully. He was handling it better now.

"You probably think I'm some kind of space cadet, don't you?" Naomi asked quietly.

"Maybe. If I knew what a space cadet was."

"I'm not some ivory-tower type, you know. I don't just teach. My work at the Institute for Human Potential Awareness is important. We even do contract work for industry."

"Industry trying to design a better man these days?" Remo asked in a dry voice.

"No, human homogeneousness is not static. Population group studies show definite phenotypical trends. For example, people's rumps are getting wider."

"I hadn't heard that," Remo said, thinking: What a space cadet.

"It's no joke. We did work for the airline industry, measuring fannies so they would know how much to widen the next generation of airline seats."

"Can't have people getting struck, now, can we?"

"Before that," Naomi went on brittley, "I did field-work. You probably never heard of the Moomba tribe."

"Not me. I can't even do the mambo."

"They were a culturally isolated group of hunter-gatherers discovered in the Philippines. I was the first woman—the first person, really—to be admitted into the Moomba secret rituals."

"Oh, yeah?" Remo said, interest flickering in his voice. "What was it like?"

"I was hoping you wouldn't ask," she said, picking through his chest hair. "Do you know in lower primates what I'm doing now would be the postcopulation checking for lice?"

"No, and I wish I was still in ignorance of that arresting fact."

"There are a lot of carryovers from primate behavior."

"Tell me about the rituals."

"Well, I've never told anyone this," Naomi said, looking up at him. "I refused to write a monograph about it. The head of the anthropology department at my last teaching position thought I had become initiated into some kind of primitive magic society, but it wasn't anything like that. I was a young, idealistic anthropologist then. I guess I couldn't get along in the modern world that well. I thought doing field-work with primitive cultures, which I had more empathy for, would work for me."

"Didn't, huh?"

"It took six months to gain the confidence of the Moomba tribe. Then one night we went into the rain forest to this circle of banyan trees. We all got naked together."

"Group sex?"

"I wish. Starting with the chief, we all took turns squatting in the center of the circle and . . . defecating into shallow wooden bowls."

"Sounds like that would be worth six months of preparation, yeah," Remo said dryly.

"That wasn't the worst of it. When everyone was done—and that included me—the chief took a so-called magic stick and measured each stool. *Mine* was the largest."

"Congratulations. Did you win a prize?"

"You might say so. They presented me with the magic stick and explained that I was now the consecrated measurer of stools."

"You lucky anthropologist, you. What happened after that?"

"That was it. That time. At the next meeting of the society, we did the same thing, only I did the measuring. Then we all sat around discussing the relative merits of one another's turds. Oh, God, this sounds so ridiculous now."

"Now?" Remo asked.

"I had gotten myself inducted into a primitive shit-appreciation society. That's *all* they did. Measure and discuss stools. When they got bored with that, they discussed color and texture and firmness of stools. Not to mention legendary stools of their ancestors. It was depressing. For years anthropologists had been speculating on the probable meaning of the ritual. It would have made my reputation, but I was too ashamed to publish my findings."

"I can see where you might be," Remo said, blank-faced.

"I was crushed. I had idealized these people as closer to nature than civilized people, imbued with elemental wisdom, and all that. And for recreation, they played with their feces like toddlers. That was it. I gave up fieldwork and ended up at U Mass with the other unemployable academics."

"Well, your story explains one thing," Remo remarked.

"What's that?"

"Why you keep trying to measure me," Remo said. "Must be a carryover from your primate ancestor experiences."

Naomi Vanderkloot had no answer to that, and Remo smiled for the first time that day.

His smile lived as long as it took him to inhale, for he happened to glance through the fern-choked window and saw a silent figure pass on the street like a figment from a dream.

Seeing the color seep from Remo's face, Naomi gasped. "What is it? What do you see?"

"A ghost," Remo said, reaching for his clothes. "As yellow and wrinkled as a raisin, and coming up your walk."

The door chimes rang and Naomi frantically scrambled for her clothes. She and Remo were dressed by the time the chimes sounded a third time. Before there could be a fourth, the rip-squeal of tortured hinges told them that they needn't bother to answer the door. It was open.

The Master of Sinanju had decided that he would not kill the woman known as Naomi Vanderkloot immediately. First he would question her about the source of her knowledge of Remo. The Nero-like Ransome had not considered that an important matter, but the Master of Sinanju knew that Smith would have made it a priority. And so would Chiun, who considered himself to be still working for Smith.

When the woman did not bother to answer the front bell, even though the sound of her respiration came clearly through the thick oval-windowed door, Chiun decided not to bother with the door. He sent it inward with a short-armed punch and stepped over it, careful not to injure his sandals on the broken glass.

A thin-faced woman with a long nose peered around a doorway molding. Her mouth flew open and she cried, "It's him! The Mongoloid!"

"Still your tongue. I am no horse Mongol come to loot and pillage. I am Korean."

"That's what I said. A Mongoloid. Do you know you carry Japanese genes?"

Chiun's eyes made walnuts at the base insult. Before he could speak, another face joined hers at the door. And this time it was Chiun's mouth that flew open in surprise.

"Remo!" he gasped.

The pair came out of the room. They walked out with their round white eyes even rounder than normal, giving them, to Chiun's eyes, comically identical expressions. The girl cowered behind Remo, as if for protection.

"You're Chiun, aren't you?" Remo asked in an uncertain voice.

"No, I am not Chiun," the Master of Sinanju snapped. Even for Remo, it was a stupid question. But to Chiun's amazement, the retort did not bring a like response. Instead, Remo descended into imbecility.

"Well," he said, "whatever your name is, I thought you were dead."

"Who told you that?" Chiun demanded.

"Nobody. I saw it in a dream."

"I have been in Sinanju. And why are you not in prison?"

"You know about that? Then you *do* know me?"

"Certainly I know you. You are Remo." Chiun hesitated. His slit eyes narrowed. Had it happened again? The thing he most dreaded? Had the spirit of Shiva once again supplanted Remo's true personality? But no, his face lacked the stern demonic cast. And he was babbling. Shiva, the Hindu God of Destruction, would never babble. Still, something was amiss.

"So you hear me, O Shatterer of Worlds?" he asked loudly.

Remo and the white woman looked at one another and then behind themselves. Seeing nothing, they returned their stupid gazes to the Master of Sinanju.

"Who are you talking to?" Remo asked.

"I wish to speak with Shiva, the Destroyer."

"That's a Hindu god," Naomi whispered. "I think."

"Never heard of him, or it," Remo hissed back.

Chiun tensed. Certainly Remo knew of Shiva. He did not remember the last time Shiva had overtaken his personality, during the time of the Japanese occupation of Arizona. And it soon had passed. But it was the fear of another such spell that had sent Chiun back to Sinanju to seek a remedy in his scrolls.

Remo would not know that either. But he knew that Shiva dwelt within him.

"You do not know Shiva?" Chiun asked padding forward. "Yet you know that you are Remo."

"Of course I'm Remo," Remo said, shaking a cigarette from his pack.

"What are you doing?" Chiun screeched, pointing to the cigarette dangling from Remo's mouth.

"Smoking a Camel," Remo replied coolly.

"You smell like you have been smoking camels—as well as cows and other malodorous creatures. But I was referring to the tobacco thing in your mouth."

Remo struck a match and lit the cigarette. Chiun reacted. He flew at Remo and plucked the cigarette from his surprised lips. He shredded it with furious finger motions.

Remo stood there in surprise. Naomi screeched and leapt behind Remo.

"Protect me, Remo!" she yelled. "He burns his sugar faster than anything I've ever seen!"

"Emperor Smith is gravely ill," Chiun said, ignoring the woman's obviously demented babbling.

"Emperor?" Remo's voice was blank.

"I wonder if he means Harold Smith?" Naomi said suddenly, peering out from behind Remo.

"Of course I mean Harold Smith," Chiun snapped. "And what do you know of Smith?"

It was Remo who answered. "He's the judge who sent me away."

Chiun blinked. In a mock-calm voice he said, "So you remember that much."

"I've had twenty years on death row to reflect on it," Remo said tartly, his tone so disrespectful that Chiun was tempted to discipline him. But the vibrations Remo gave off, as Chiun stood close to him, were wrong. They were not Remo's vibrations, nor Shiva's. They were . . . off.

"Twenty years," Chiun said. "You mean twenty days, do you not?"

"No, I mean twenty years."

"I have had the misfortune to train you for more than twenty years, and I know where you have been. And it is not in prison."

"Then it's true. The dreams."

"Tell me of these dreams," Chiun demanded.

"You and I. We were doing incredible, impossible things. And Smith was in the dreams. And a place called Folcroft."

"Those were not dreams, but a reality you have somehow lost," Chiun said sagely.

"If that's so, then why did you let me languish in prison?"

"I returned to Sinanju to attend certain matters, and while I was sojourning there, the new emperor informed me that you had returned to prison on an undercover assignment."

"Undercover!" Remo burst out. "I was almost buried there."

"What do you mean?"

"I was on death row!" Remo said hotly. "They had me scheduled for execution at seven o'clock this morning. I went over the wall."

The Master of Sinanju indicated the woman with a fingernail like an ivory spear.

"And this woman," he said slowly. "How is she part of this wild story of yours—aside from your usual reason?"

"What's my usual reason?"

Chiun's nose wrinkled in distaste. "Sex."

"I resent that insinuation," Naomi Vanderkloot said sharply. "I'll have you know that I'm a full professor."

"Although I must admit that she is more attractive than your usual cowlike consorts," Chiun added.

Remo looked at Naomi. "She is?" he said incredulously. Naomi shot him a hurt look.

Chiun asked, "You are the woman Naomi Vanderfloot?"

"Kloot. Vanderkloot. It's Dutch."

"I do not differentiate between peas," Chiun sniffed, "although some are less green than others. It is the same with Europeans. You have forbidden knowledge of Folcroft, which you are spreading in newspapers. How did you come into possession of this knowledge? Speak truthfully, for your life depends upon this."

"He told me," Naomi said, indicating Remo.

"Yeah, I told her," Remo said. "What is Folcroft anyway? I keep dreaming of it. And you."

"Do you remember Sinanju, Remo?"

"No. What is it?"

"A gift," Chiun said sadly. "Of which you are seldom worthy." And the Master of Sinanju began to turn in place, his saffron kimono skirts belled up and out like a parachute. He caught flashing glimpses of Remo simply standing there like any common white oaf, the woman cowering behind him.

And Chiun struck.

Remo's hands shot up instinctively as he dropped into a defensive crouch. One of Chiun's sandaled feet snapped out, and although the blow was restrained, it sent Remo spinning. At the last possible moment, Remo had parried the blow with one wrist.

Chiun alighted and pushed his skirts down as Remo, his face shocked white, slowly gained his feet. He bowed.

"Your mind may not remember Sinanju," he said solemnly, "but your body does. And for that I give thanks to my ancestors."

"Know anything about what he's saying?" Remo asked Naomi, not taking his eyes off the Master of Sinanju.

"Asians are culturally fixated on ancestor worship," Naomi said quietly. "But the rest of it must be some belief system. That's cultural anthropology. I don't do cultural anthropology any more." Raising her voice, she asked, "What do you want here?"

"I have been sent to kill you."

"Over my dead body," Remo snapped, returning to his crouch as Naomi slipped behind him. She grabbed the back of his T-shirt in nervous fistfuls, and Chiun noticed for the first time that it was neither stark white nor jet black, but a pleasing saffron. He wondered if this Remo might not be an improvement over the old.

"Your body is already dead," Chiun said. "For you are the dead night tiger of Sinanju legend, the avatar of Shiva. I could, if you wish, show you the grave where your government buried you."

"I knew it!" Naomi snapped. "It's a government plot. It's—" Her face went white. Her mouth made shapes but no sounds.

"Spit it out," Remo prompted. "What are you trying to say?"

"A clone!" Naomi shrilled. "The real Remo is dead, and you're a genetic clone of him created by the

CIA. Not an evolutionary mutant. You're probably filled with yucky artificial ingredients. Oh, my God, I slept with a clone. What will my mother think!"

Remo looked toward Chiun. "Any idea what a clone is?"

"No, but it does not matter. Listen to me, Remo. Do you wish to know the truth about yourself?"

"Yeah."

"Will you accompany me to Folcroft, where the answers lie?"

"What do you think, Naomi?"

Naomi backed away. "Don't even speak to me, you . . . you impostor!"

"What about her?" Remo asked.

"If she agrees to accompany us, she will not be killed."

"Well, I've come this far," Naomi said abruptly. "I'll see this through to the end."

"That is laudable," Chiun said with a tight wise smile. "Come, let us be on our way while there is still light."

The Master of Sinanju stepped aside for the two whites to lead. They hesitated, then, seeing the elfin twinkle that he allowed to come into his clear hazel eyes, they stepped past him. Remo pushed the nervous woman along with his hands on her shoulders.

At the precise moment that they passed him, the Master of Sinanju tripped Remo. Remo went down like a sack of potatoes. The woman shrank back but she was not swift enough to elude the talonlike fingers that reached up for her long-necked throat.

A moment's pressure on the base of the neck was sufficient. Her eyes rolled up in her head and she vented a sigh. Then she collapsed to the floor like a deflating balloon.

Chiun stepped back and put his hands into his joined sleeves as Remo, his face horrified, knelt at the woman's side.

"You little fraud, she's not breathing!" Remo said, looking up in anger.

"She breathes poorly, but she breathes," Chiun told him unconcernedly.

Remo placed a hand over her heart, and feeling a beat, let out his pent breath. The tightness in his face loosened.

"Now what?" he demanded tightly. "Are you going to sandbag me next?"

"Now that she will not interfere, you and I will go to Folcroft."

Remo stood up, his hands bone-white fists of tension. "No more tricks?"

"Not from me," Chiun said loftily.

"Then you go first," Remo said, motioning for the Master of Sinanju to lead the way, which Chiun was only too happy to do. For night was coming on, and miles away, at Folcroft Sanitarium, there was much to be done, and many matters to settle.

Particularly with the new director of CURE, Norvell Ransome.

23

Norvell Ransome's watery eyes registered momentary shock as Remo and Chiun entered his office. Then a studied calmness dropped over them like a dingy veil.

"Remo Williams, dear boy!" he exclaimed. "What an astonishing turn of events. You two have obviously found one another."

"*I* found Remo," Chiun said, closing the door. Remo stepped off to one side, his dark eyes unreadable.

"And the Vanderkloot woman?" Ransome inquired. It was almost a purr.

"I dealt with her as Smith would have wished," Chiun said. "She will trouble us no longer."

"Smith was—I mean is—an exceedingly efficient administrator. I know he would be pleased." Ransome cleared his throat with a rumble of phlegm. He touched the concealed stud under the lip of the desk and the CURE terminal disappeared silently, a blank panel sliding over its well.

"I imagine, Remo, that you would like an explanation for your recent incarceration," Ransome said unctuously.

Remo started to speak, but the Master of Sinanju shushed him with a knifelike gesture.

"*We* would like an explanation," Chiun said pointedly.

"To be sure." Norvell Ransome laid his pudgy fingers flatly on the desk. This was a critical moment. Chiun had found Remo and brought him back, as he had expected. The question remained, how much did Remo remember? And how would he react?

"You are aware that the security of this operation requires extraordinary measures," Ransome began. "Especially measures in the event of compromise or catastrophic failure. Failure such as the compromising of this facility, or the death or exposure of one of its operatives."

"We know this," Chiun intoned.

Carefully Ransome lifted a copy of the *National Enquirer* from the desk drawer and held up the front page, showing the artistic likeness of Remo's face.

"You both know of Smith's unfortunate situation," he continued. "It was brought about by this regrettable display of journalistic excess. Hence the need to remove the Vanderkloot woman. This presented the

President with a conundrum. To shut down CURE operations? Or to await Smith's recovery and decide upon a course of action later? The President, I am pleased to report, resorted to the latter option. That is where I came in. My first instruction was to set into motion Operation RESTORE, which is one of Smith's rather ingenious, ah, retirement programs. I must say that this presented me with an unaccustomed challenge, but it was made much easier by your fortuitous absence, Master Chiun."

"Are we going to listen to this windbag all night?" Remo demanded. "He's not giving us squat."

"Hush," Chiun admonished. "Forgive my pupil. He has been testy since his recent brush with death."

Ransome let that pass with a simple "Ah." He continued, "It was as simple as waiting until Remo was in the comfort of his very own domicile. A home which, I am sorry to inform you at this late date, Dr. Smith had the foresight to tamper with in certain subtle ways. In short, Mr. Williams, you were gassed in your sleep."

"Impossible!" Chiun snapped. "No vapor could catch Remo unawares."

"A colorless, odorless gas that insinuated itself into his bedroom while he slept," Ransome quickly inserted. "Remo was removed here to Folcroft by ambulance, where, still sedated, his memory was, I regret to say, tampered with. It is very complicated, but it involves a certain drug that wipes the memory clean, going back to any point the administrator—and I use the term advisedly—chooses. Rather like erasing a portion of audio tape. Artificial memories are substituted via posthypnotic suggestion. For Smith evidently felt that some memories might not suppress successfully. So they were transformed. I reviewed the computerized memory simulations before the Folcroft doctors—who thought they were conducting a modest experiment—and was quite stunned.

If you remembered Smith, you would recall him as Judge Smith. A deceased CURE operative named MacCleary became the fodder for a simulated memory involving the murder of a prison guard who never existed. And if you remembered Chiun—Smith's greatest fear—you would trigger a memory of his unfortunate demise. After that, you were transferred from here, using altered documents. The rest you know. You woke up on Florida's unparalleled death row, unaware that you had not spent the previous two decades at the New Jersey correctional facility, which was the last true recollection you were allowed to retain."

"You smarmy bastard!" Remo said, starting forward. Chiun stopped him with a hand placed to his chest.

"Please," Norvell Ransome said, "restrain yourself. This was Dr. Smith's program. I merely, ah, executed it."

"And the state of Florida nearly executed me," Remo snarled.

"What?"

"I was scheduled to die this morning."

"Dear me. Is this true, Master Chiun?"

"If Remo says it is true, it is true," Chiun returned coolly.

"This was most unfortunate. Some bureaucratic malfeasance, for which the responsible parties will pay dearly, let me assure you. You see, it was all very elegant, but quite harmless. Remo, without memory of CURE or Folcroft or any of it, was simply deposited back in the place where he came from— death row. A facility other than Trenton State was mandated, of course, because Remo Williams had been executed at Trenton. Or so it is believed."

"Then Haines *was* telling the truth," Remo gasped.

Ransome's open face contracted suddenly. "Haines?"

"The state executioner who was to pull the switch

on me. The same one who did it years before,"
Remo said.

"Really? The same executioner? Remarkable."

"Dreadful," Chiun corrected. "We nearly lost
Remo."

"That was not the intent of Project RESTORE, let
me assure you." Globules of sweat were breaking out
on Ransome's forehead now. One ran down one side
of his nose and dripped into his open mouth. He
swallowed it absently. "The plan was simply to keep
Remo out of the public eye while Dr. Smith's situation became clear. For you see, this particular plan
suited both problems: Smith's illness and the *Enquirer*
exposure."

"What was supposed to happen to me if Smith
didn't recover?"

"My dear man, you must understand me when I tell
you that the answer to that question is classified. Who
knows, but Dr. Smith or I may have to implement it at
some future point." And Norvell Ransome broke out into
bubbling laughter. It shook his bulky toadlike form,
but left the Master of Sinanju and Remo unmoved.

Ransome subsided.

"Truthfully, that would be up to the President,"
Ransome said in a subdued voice. "Remo's memory
is easily restored in the event Smith's possible demise
does not effectively shut us down."

"Well, now that we're all here," Remo said suspiciously, "what now?"

"Now," Ransome said, glancing at his wristwatch,
"it is growing late." He pushed himself up from his
desk. "I anticipated Master Chiun's return, but not
yours, Remo. A room has been prepared for you,
and let me suggest you take advantage of it. For the
night is no longer young."

"I'm not sure I trust this guy," Remo said, causing
a hurt expression to settle over Ransome's corpulent
face.

"Remo," Chiun hissed. "Shame on you. You have heard this man's reasonable explanation." Ransome's face brightened. "Let us take advantage of his generous hospitality. Tomorrow will be time enough to discuss the pressing matter of our future. And CURE's."

"Excellent. Let me escort you to your room personally. Would you object to taking the elevator down? It's on the first floor."

Without waiting for an answer, Norvell Ransome led the way. The flooring shook with his thunderous tread.

"I've seen fat before," Remo whispered to Chiun, "but this bag of lard is an elephant. And his explanation may seen reasonable to you, but it sounds fishy to me. Take it from a guy who knows all there is to know about cons and con jobs."

Chiun said nothing as they rode the elevator to the first floor.

"Whew!" Remo said as they stepped out. "Good thing we had the elevator. Walking down an entire flight of steps is more than I'm up to tonight."

His sarcasm was ignored by Chiun and Ransome.

Ransome led them to a room in the patient wing. It was large, but sparsely furnished. Chiun recognized it as quarters he had occupied in times when he lived at Folcroft.

"There are sleeping mats and a television, as you can see," Ransome was saying. "I will have dinner sent down if you wish. Would you like a menu?"

"Just rice for me," Remo said, bringing a delighted smile to Chiun's parchment visage.

"And rice for me as well," Chiun added.

"Excellent," Norvell Ransome said, "It will be served presently. Now, if you will excuse me, I must bid you both a pleasant good night."

After Ransome had gone, Remo looked at the solitary sleeping mats and, thinking of Naomi's futon, asked, "Doesn't anyone sleep on beds anymore?"

Chiun's answer was lost in hissing white clouds spurting from the wallboards on every side.

It looked like steam but it bit the skin like dry ice.

The Master of Sinanju reacted instantly. But instantly was too late, for his limbs were quick-frozen at once, like a TV dinner. He fell, one elbow and a bent knee preventing his rigid body from touching the floor.

Remo fell straight back, his hands on his hips. He hit like a board, still and unyielding. His face was as white as a snowman's. He's still-open eyes stared blindly, the pupils frozen with a dusting of opaque ice.

And out in the corridor, Norvell Ransome turned the hand wheel marked "Liquid Nitrogen" and closed the wall panel concealing it.

He took the elevator back to his office, suddenly regretting that he had not thought to ask either of them what the acronym CURE had stood for. Well, the night was young. Perhaps the computers would finally give up that most stubborn secret.

After all, CURE had surrendered everything else of value. Including its most potent human weapons.

The too-brief sensation of weightlessness ceased and brought Norvell Ransome's bulk back down to earth. He stepped past the sliding elevator doors and into the dim corridor, where he spied a peripheral flicker of movement and felt a slight breath of disturbed air.

A fire door was closing, and beyond it came the soft pad of feet on stairs. Norvell Ransome went to the door and opened it. He peered down. The stairwell was empty.

"Security guard, no doubt," he told himself. Then he waddled back to the office, intending to call the captain of the guards about the annoying irregularity.

He had ordered rigorously timed tours of the building and grounds.

Norvell Ransome eased himself into the cracked leather chair and reached for the blue telephone. He stopped, his hand frozen over the receiver. It quivered as his eyes drank in the sight of the CURE terminal screen, up from its well like a blank-faced robot.

"What the devil," he said under his breath. He was certain he had returned it to its well before leaving. It was standard CURE security procedure, which he adhered to religiously.

Ransome blinked. In the exact middle of the screen, a short string of glowing green letters floated.

Ransome leaned closer. When he read the words, every muscle in his face went slack. His jaw dropped, giving him two extra chins. He swore aloud, but all that came out was a froggy croak.

For the words on the screen constituted a simple message: I AM BACK.

24

Dr. Alan Dooley crept down the third-floor corridor to Folcroft's hospital wing. He slipped into Dr. Smith's room, his eyes haunted.

Smith lay under the oxygen tent. He was the color of fish skin, Dr. Dooley saw. His lips and fingernails were gray. Not blue. They had been a faint blue just minutes ago. Smith was improving. Dooley couldn't understand how.

He stepped up to the plastic tenting and rustled it. Smith's eyes fluttered open. "It's me, Dooley," Dooley told him. "I did exactly as you asked. It was easy, once I located the status key."

"What did computer say?" Smith's words were a croak.

"The words were PALLIATIVE. RESTORE. FREEZE-DRY"

"PALLIATIVE," Smith muttered dryly. "That means he's sanctioned. And you say he ordered you to ignore my medical needs?"

"Not in so many words," Dooley admitted. "But it was clear that he preferred that you never recover. He forbade any significant medical intervention, such as an operation. When I insisted, he sent me away. But my conscience bothered me. I relieved the other doctor."

"You are not part of the Folcroft staff," Smith said.

"I was on staff of New York City Hospital. Ransome contacted me. Insisted I resign and come to work here. He . . . he knew some things about me. I don't know how it's possible, but he did."

"The computer told him," Smith said.

"What kind of computer would know—"

"—that you are a suspected child molester?" Dr. Dooley started. "The less you know," Smith added, "the better off you will be. Now let me think. RESTORE means that Remo is out of the picture. FREEZE-DRY can only mean he's used the liquid-nitrogen room. He's very smart. He must have neutralized Chiun." Smith's voice lifted. "Dooley. Listen carefully. Go to the first floor, the dormitory wing. You will find a wall panel outside Room Fifty-five. Open it and depress the red button. Wait one hour and Room Fifty-five will open automatically. Assist the individual you will find inside. Inform him that you are acting on my behalf. Then bring him to me. Is that understood?"

"Yes. I think."

"Now, go. Ransome will be puzzled by the message you left on the terminal. This will be the first place he will look."

Dr. Dooley withdrew from the room. He started for the elevator, but the indicator light winked on. Someone was about to step off the lift. Dooley ducked back and slipped through a fire exit leading to the stairwell.

Norvell Ransome stepped off the elevator. It was most distressing, he ruminated. The CURE computer had been accessed. Remo and Chiun were out of the picture. That left only Smith.

Ransome hesitated outside Smith's door. What if this was a lure of some kind? Physical danger was not one of Norvell Ransome's loves in life. It was the reason why, when the government combed Ivy League universities in the 1960's for members of prominent old-line families, Norvell Ransome of the Virginia Ransomes opted for the NSA and not the CIA. Guns were the first resort of the intellectually limited.

Taking a deep breath, Ransome pushed open the door. Smith lay inert, apparently unchanged from hours before. He approached the bedside cautiously, noticing the absence of blue from Smith's lips and nails. They gave him a deathlier cast, but a glance at the heart monitor oscilloscope indicated a steady heartbeat. Smith's sunken chest continued to rise and fall with his faint breathing.

No, Norvell Ransome decided, Dr. Harold W. Smith had not been the interloper. It was not his nature to boldly proclaim his return with the childish statement "I am back."

Ransome hurried from the room, thinking: Who? Only four persons were supposed to know of CURE's existence. Its three operatives were contained. That left only the President, but he was hardly a likely candidate. Yet someone with knowledge of CURE was prowling Folcroft. It must be one of the secrets in the hidden files, along with the meaning of the acronym CURE.

This time Ransome impatiently suffered through the elevator descent. There was nothing to make the blood course through the body like a good mystery.

Dr. Alan Dooley was surprised when at last the door to Room 55 opened and he found two individuals on the floor. They lay there like grotesque discarded mannequins. The walls radiated a strong warmth. Dooley had noticed the hand wheel marked "Liquid Nitrogen" and understood. These men had been quick-frozen by the only substance known to do it safely without cellular damage. They probably never knew what hit them. Dooley shivered in the warmth as he knelt and raised their eyelids. He passed a hand over their pupils, intercepting the light. He got reactions from both men. Good.

"Wake up," Dooley hissed, slapping the white man. "Come on," he urged. The white man did not respond, but the Asian began to stir on his own. He sat up suddenly, his eyes fierce.

"I'm Dr. Dooley. Smith sent me."

"I am interested in the one called Ransome," the Asian said coldly. Then he noticed the other man. "Remo!" he said, shocked.

"He's okay. It's just taking him longer to come around. You were quick-frozen."

As the Asian ministered to the other man, he said, "And I promise you that the fate that awaits that elephant will not be quick, but infinitely slow."

Faster than Dooley thought was possible, the Asian brought the man he called Remo around. Remo sat up, blinking dully.

"What happened?" Remo demanded. "I remember a kind of fog, then nothing."

"I will explain later. We must go with this man. Come."

They made their way up the stairwell to Smith's bedside.

Smith didn't react until Dooley rustled the oxygen tent. Only then did his eyes snap open.

"Master Chiun," he said. Then, startled: "Remo! What are you doing here?"

"I broke jail," Remo said coldly. "Chiun explained who you really are. I work for you, he says. But I remember you as the guy who sent me to death row."

"There will be time enough for explanations later," Smith said uncomfortably.

"Not for me. I've had enough of this craziness. I hereby give my notice. See you in the want ads."

Remo started for the door. He found himself on his stomach instead, the old Oriental standing on his solar plexus. He bounced slightly, forcing air in and out of Remo's lungs. It hurt, but surprisingly, his brain began to clear. He decided he liked breathing through the stomach.

"Do not listen to Remo, Emperor," Chiun was saying. "He has not been himself since he was nearly executed again."

"Again?" Smith asked, looking toward Dooley. The doctor's brow furrowed.

"The pretender called Ransome arranged for Remo to be executed in my absence," Chiun explained.

"Then he *is* a rogue element," Smith muttered. "Sanctioned or not, he must be stopped."

"I will be happy to attend to that detail," Chiun said.

"No!" Smith hissed. "He is still the President's man. Eliminating him would only create problems. It must appear to be an accident."

"I have many excellent accidents in my repertoire," Chiun said, beaming.

"No. I have a contingency plan for this situation, as well. I want one of you to penetrate my office while the other distracts Ransome. Lift the blue telephone and push the loudness lever underneath to the highest position."

"Remo can do that. It is simple enough," Chiun said quickly. He looked down. "Is that all right with you, Remo?"

"It is if someone will get off my stomach," Remo replied.

The Master of Sinanju stepped off and Remo got to his feet. His eyes were clearer.

"I meant what I said about quitting," Remo told Smith. "Judge."

Smith ignored him and addressed Chiun. "I am told there are special guards now attached to Folcroft."

"I have already dealt with the worst of them."

"Kill them all," Smith croaked.

"Good God," Dr. Dooley blurted. "What is this all about?"

"We cannot take a chance that Ransome has allowed them to know too much," Smith added.

"How much is too much?" Dr. Dooley said hoarsely, looking from face to face. He stopped and did a double-take on Remo. "Have I seen you before?" he asked. "Your face looks familiar."

"Ever read the *National Enquirer*?" Remo asked.

"Of course not!"

"Liar," Remo snapped.

"Dr. Dooley," Smith interrupted, "I will require a telephone and a wheelchair."

"I'm sorry. As your physician, I strongly advise against exerting yourself."

"You are an employee of this facility," Smith said coldly. "And I am its director. You will do as I say."

The force in Smith's voice stopped Dr. Dooley's

next words. The long fingernails of the Asian called
Chiun suddenly floating up to his face helped too.
Dooley left hurriedly.

"Well, what are you waiting for?" Smith asked
Remo.

"Directions. How the hell would I know where
your office is?"

"Oh," Smith said. "I had forgotten. Master Chiun,
will you direct him, please?"

"Yes. We will return shortly," Chiun said, bowing.

Remo and Chiun left. After the door closed, Dr.
Harold W. Smith closed his eyes. It was a strain to
speak, but despite the expenditure of effort, he was
feeling better.

From the corridor, Remo's voice drifted back. "Explain
something to me, will you? If you work for
Smith, why does he call you master?"

Norvell Ransome ignored the beeping lights on his
computer, warning of developing national-security
and domestic concerns. Time enough for those matters
later. There must be a hidden file in the Folcroft
data base. He brought up the system's diagnostic
program and began scanning the dump. Lines of raw
data sped by his eager eyes, showing a mixture of
hexidecimal codes and plain ASCII—readable text.

To his befuddlement, he found no hidden files, no
breath of a clue to the identity of the mysterious
interloper. And worst of all to his inquisitive mind,
the riddle of the CURE acronym remained unexplained.

The intercom buzzed. Annoyance on his face,
Ransome reached for the button.

"What is it, Mrs. Mikulka?" he asked petutantly.
And then it hit him. Eileen Mikulka, Smith's secretary.
Perhaps she . . .

But all such suspicions fled his mind when Mrs.
Mikulka said breathlessly, "The captain of the

guards is reporting a disturbance in the gym, Mr. Ransome."

"Order all security personnel to deal with it," he barked.

"That's the problem. The guard force are already in the gym. And they're requesting reinforcements. Should I call the police?"

"Absolutely not! What is the nature of the disturbance?"

"They're so frantic I can't get that out of them."

"I see," Ransome said slowly. "Thank you for bringing this to my attention, Mrs. Mikulka. I shall see to the matter personally."

Norvell Ransome ignored her as he bounded past her desk. His tread made the water in her desktop flower vase slop over the lip and onto the Rolodex.

Mrs. Eileen Mikulka felt nervous. Since Dr. Smith's heart attack—if that was indeed his problem—nothing had seemed to go right. She thought the whole matter of Norvell Ransome himself was very strange. The lecherous way he looked at the nurses. She had even caught him looking at her in a disturbingly carnal way.

Then a stranger thing happened. A man she knew only as Remo, who had worked at Folcroft in some custodial capacity months before, emerged from the stairwell, looking lost.

"Hi!" he said nervously. "Is this Dr. Smith's office?"

"Of course," she replied. "You know that, Mr. . . . I'm afraid I've forgotten your name."

"Thanks. Just checking," he said, slipping into the office.

"Wait!" she called after him. "You can't go in there." She started to rise from her desk, but the door lock clicked. He had locked it after him.

Something was distinctly wrong, but Mrs. Eileen

Mikulka was not about to do anything to get herself fired. She composed herself and waited for Mr. Ransome's return.

Inside Dr. Smith's office, Remo walked up to the desk and lifted the ordinary blue telephone. It was a standard AT&T model. Underneath there was a silver lever. He slid it to the end of the slot marked "Louder."

That done, he paused for a look around the Spartan office. There was a big picture window behind the desk, showing Long Island Sound. None of it looked familiar to him. But it exactly matched the office Smith had occupied in one of his dreams. Puzzled, Remo hurried to the door.

Norvell Ransome approached the big black double doors to the Folcroft gym. He put his ear to the cold metal. There was absolutely no sound on the other side. Ransome procrastinated. This was not to his taste at all. Dealing with physical problems like a common field agent. That was why he had hired a fresh complement of guards. But summoning the police was out of the question.

With painstaking slowness he pushed the door open a crack. He peered inside.

There was a guard lying on his back on the Nautilus machine. His hand clutched the bar of the device that was weighted with heavy metal slabs. Ransome waited for him to push them up. But the guard simply held that position.

Ransome pushed the door open all the way. He saw the other guards. Two hung from gymnast hoops. Not by their hands, but by their necks, their faces a smoky lavender. Ransome gasped in spite of himself.

His entire guard force was dead. Some grotesquely so. The hanging guards, for example, had had their heads somehow forced through the aluminum rings. The rings were obviously too small for their necks, which was why their faces were purple, yet their heads had evidently gone through without crushing their skulls. The guard under the weights was literally under them. His head had been crushed, his hands clutching the handles in a death grip.

The others were worse. Yet there was no blood anywhere. Just mangled bodies. And neither was there any indication of who—or what—had decimated them.

Ransome hurried from the gym. This wing of Folcroft lacked an elevator, forcing him to run. He was puffing by the time he reached the main building. The reception-area guard was absent. Ransome assumed he had been the unfortunate with the mashed cranium.

Ransome reached the elevator in safety and stabbed the button marked two.

Mrs. Mikulka started like a frightened animal when Ransome appeared on the second floor.

"What is it now, Mrs. Mikulka?" he snapped.

"A man barged into your office. I couldn't stop him."

Ransome stopped in his tracks. "Where is he now?"

"I don't know. He left just moments ago."

"Is anyone in there now?" Ransome demanded nervously.

"No."

"Then be good enough to inform any callers that I am out for the day."

"Of course, Mr. Ransome."

Norvell Ransome locked the office door after him. He lumbered for the computer, which was up and running. Then he realized he had forgotten to conceal it this time. He frowned. Such sloppiness was unforgivable.

"Must get a grip on myself," he said, sliding behind the desk. He attacked the keyboard. Somewhere there must be a hidden file. He initiated another diagnostic dump.

The intercom buzzed and Ransome shouted, "I told you I am not accepting calls!" without bothering to trip the intercom.

"I . . . I think you should take this one," Mrs. Mikulka shouted back.

Ransome blinked. He eyed the blue telephone. Gingerly he lifted it.

"Hello?" he said cautiously.

An unfamiliar lemony voice spoke into his ear.

"It is over, Ransome. I am back."

"Who . . . who are you?"

"That you will never know. There is a contingency for everything in this organization. You should know that by now. After all, every secret of this institution is at your fingertips."

"Not quite," Ransome blurted out. "There is you, and the meaning of the organization's code name. I don't suppose I can pry that out of you?"

There was a pause on the other end. Then the lemony voice resumed speaking. "The answer to that and other questions you have may be obtained by calling a certain number."

"I have a pen in my hand," Ransome said quickly.

The lemony voice gave a phone number. Then, abruptly, the man hung up, saying, "Good-bye, Ransome."

"Wait! What about—?"

Ransome replaced the receiver. He looked at the telephone number. It bore a local exchange. In fact, it seemed familiar somehow, but he couldn't quite place it. After taking a few deep breaths to calm himself, Norvell Ransome began punching the keypad with his fat stubby fingers.

He clapped the receiver to his ear and waited for

the first ring. As his watery eyes jerked around the room nervously, he noticed the number in the plastic window under the blue telephone's keypad.

It was identical to the number he had dialed.

"What on earth!" he muttered. Then, fear rising from his Brobdingnagian belly, he hastily let go of the receiver.

The problem was that he could not. His muscles would not respond. There was a sudden sharp whiff of something burning in his nose. He never realized that it was his own nostril hairs because the neurons of his brain had died and his corneas turned cataract white from the two thousand volts coursing through his blubbery body. He continued jerking and spasming even after he had been cooked to death.

Then the lights blew and his face hit the desk edge with a mushy *whump*!

25

Folcroft Sanitarium was blacked out for no more than forty-five seconds before the emergency generators came on, filling Dr. Smith's hospital room with harsh white light. The oscilloscope beeped into life, but it did not register Smith's heart rate, for Smith was no longer hooked up to it.

Instead, he was sitting on an aluminum wheelchair, a robe covering his thin legs.

"What happened?" Remo wanted to know.

"Ransome used the telephone," Smith said tersely.

"You really should have better wiring," Remo remarked.

"The wiring is fine. Now, would one of you please push me to the elevator. We are going to reclaim my office."

Chiun turned to Remo. "Remo, do as Emperor Smith says."

"Emperor?" Remo and Dr. Dooley said simultaneously.

"Now," Chiun added sharply.

Obligingly Remo got behind Smith and started pushing. Chiun and Dr. Dooley followed them to the elevator. They rode one floor down in silence.

Mrs. Eileen Mikulka jumped to her feet at the sight of her employer being wheeled up to her desk.

"Dr. Smith!" she exclaimed.

"Mrs. Mikulka, you have the rest of the day off," Smith said firmly, his gray eyes on the closed door to his office.

Mrs. Mikulka didn't ask questions. She grabbed her purse and ran.

The Master of Sinanju took the lead. He found the door locked. He placed both palms to the panel and exerted what seemed to the others like testing pressure.

In response, the door groaned metallically and fell inward.

Remo rolled Smith over the horizontal panel, remarking to Chiun, "You really have a way with doors, you know that?"

"It is Sinanju," Chiun returned. "Something obviously beyond your white mentality."

Once inside, everyone fell silent as they absorbed the sight of Norvell Ransome collapsed behind the desk.

Remo smelled the air. "Smells like burning hair."

"That is one result of death by electrocution,"

Smith said while Dr. Dooley placed a hand over Ransome's fat-sheathed heart. Feeling nothing, he shifted to the carotid artery. He looked up.

"This man is dead," he said hoarsely.

Noticing that Ransome clutched a half-melted telephone receiver in one hand, Remo asked of Smith, "What happened to him?"

"He dialed the wrong number."

"Yeah?" Remo said slowly. "I don't suppose this has anything to to with that lever you had me throw?"

"It armed the telephone."

"Armed?" Remo said blankly. "How do you arm a telephone?"

"By pushing the little lever, of course," Chiun said impatiently. "Emperor, shall I remove the garbage?"

"How can you talk of garbage at a time like this?" Remo asked.

No one answered him. The Master of Sinanju stepped behind the desk. He plucked something from one voluminous sleeve and lifted Ransome's slack face up by the hair. Chiun affixed a Band-Aid to the still-steaming forehead. Written across it were the words DO NOT RESUSCITATE. He pushed the leather chair away and into a closet, Norvell Ransome's corpulent body—still clutching the half-melted receiver—jiggling with an almost boneless animation.

"Looks like he got the same medicine he tried to feed me," Remo said as the closet door was shut on the corpse.

At Smith's signal, Chiun pushed the wheelchair behind the desk. Smith wordlessly opened a drawer and pulled out a red telephone. He lifted the receiver and waited.

Presently he said, "Mr. President, this is Harold W. Smith. I am calling to inform you of the accidental death of my temporary replacement, Norvell Ransome." Smith paused. "He was electrocuted attempting to tamper with areas of our computer sys-

tem he was not authorized to access. . . . Yes, it is
regrettable. Yes, I am prepared to resume my former responsibilities if you will sanction continued
CURE operations."

Smith listened as he waited. "Thank you, Mr.
President, I will report as soon as all the loose ends
are cleared up."

Smith hung up, grim-faced.

"Master Chiun," he said coldly. "How compromised are we?"

"The woman named Vanderkloot knows of Folcroft,
but not of CURE."

"I see."

Smith's gray eyes fell upon Remo Williams. "And
you, Remo. Who knows you still exist?"

Remo considered. "Naomi. Haines. He's the guy
who executed me once and almost got a second
chance. The prison warden. And I'd say, oh, maybe
two thousand hardened convicts, give or take a few."
Remo's smile was dark and taunting.

"Hmmmm," Smith was saying. "Other than Haines,
how many of these know you were executed years
ago?"

"Just Haines, as far as I know. Why?"

"Because all serious security risks must be neutralized as rapidly as possible," Smith said. He was
looking past Remo. Remo turned around. Dr. Alan
Dooley stood helplessly, his eyes sick.

"Chiun," Smith said quietly.

"As you wish, Emperor," the Master of Sinanju
said, advancing on Dr. Dooley.

"What's he going to do?" Remo asked anxiously.

Dr. Dooley shrank back against a wall. "Wait, you
can't do this. I helped you, Smith. I saved your life."

"No," Chiun corrected. "I saved his life. I im-
parted new strength so that his heart could heal
itself."

"But I'm on your side, Smith!" Dr. Dooley whim-

pered. He was afraid of the old Asian. He didn't
know why. He was ancient. Frail. But those oblique
hazel eyes filled him with dread.

"Wait a minute," Remo said, horrified. He addressed Smith. "How can you kill him? What did he
ever do except help you out?"

"Make it quick and painless," Smith said, "even
though the man is a child molester."

"A defiler of children!" squeaked Chiun. He was
standing before the cowering doctor now.

"But I helped you!" Dooley screeched. "All of
you!"

The Master of Sinanju's hands, nail-headed hydras,
transfixed Dr. Alan Dooley. One homed in on his
staring face. It filled his vision. He never saw the
other hand disappear. It drove in once, into his
heart, and pulled back so fast the nails were clear of
blood. Dr. Dooley's face registered uncomprehending
shock. He looked down. Over his heart, five bright
scarlet dots grew into spots and spread in all directions, forming an unstoppable red stain.

Dr. Alan Dooley crumpled at the Master of Sinanju's
unconcerned feet.

"Jesus Christ!" Remo said, turning on Smith. "You
are the most cold-blooded son of a bitch I've ever
seen outside of the can. That guy saved your butt.
Or doesn't that count for anything?"

"He knew too much. And he had been targeted for
exposure and probable prison. This was a better fate
than prison would have been, don't you agree?"

"Whatever happened to due process?" Remo wanted
to know. His fists were clenched in anger.

"Sometimes circumstances force us to make excep-
tions," Smith told him sadly, "so that due process
can be maintained for the majority of Americans.
That is the purpose of CURE. Ransome, for all his
access to our secrets, missed that point. He thought
CURE was an acronym. It is not. CURE is simply

that—a cure for America's ills. If our work is allowed to continue to its ultimate end, CURE will cease to exist because the need for CURE will have ended. That is our goal. No one must be allowed to stand in the way of that goal."

"So what about me?" Remo said angrily. "Back to prison—or are you going to snuff me too?"

"Chiun," Smith said tonelessly, looking Remo in the eye. "You know what to do."

"Not without a fight," Remo warned. He whirled. He never completed the turn. A hand at the back of his neck squeezed and his vision clouded over like a fast-moving line squall. . . .

Remo awoke suddenly. He was strapped down in a big steel-and-leather chair studded with dials and cables. And looking at him with clinical detachment, sitting in his wheelchair, was Dr. Harold W. Smith.

Oh, Christ, he thought. That bastard Smith is going to fry me himself. Remo tried to turn his head. When it wouldn't move, he became conscious of a band of metal encircling his neck, restraining him. He frowned, wondering what kind of electric chair went around the neck, not the temple.

"See you in hell, Smith," he grated. Smith gestured in such a way that Remo became aware that there was someone beside him, hovering at the edge of his field of vision.

Then the neckband popped. Remo jerked his head free. Someone reached over and lifted the domelike helmet that had covered his head. It was an unfamiliar man in hospital green. A doctor. Wordlessly he undid the straps that pinioned Remo's wrists, biceps, and ankles.

Remo looked around. The room was filled with complicated electronic equipment, computers, and wheeled control stations. Everything, it seemed, was connected to the chair by coaxial cable or wiring.

Chiun stood off to one side, watching him with the cocked head inquisitiveness of a terrier.

"Please leave us alone with the subject, Doctor," Smith said tonelessly.

The doctor complied and swiftly left the room.

Remo got out of the chair, rubbing his wrists.

"What do you remember, Remo?" Smith asked dryly.

Remo blinked. It was as if his brain had been cleaned of the foglike heaviness that he hadn't been able to shake since Florida State.

"All of it," Remo said bitterly. "Mostly how you rigged my very own house so you could dispose of me like used facial tissue."

"When you joined the organization, you understood that we were all expendable."

"Except me, of course," Chiun put in smugly.

"You're siding with Smith on this?" Remo accused. "I don't believe it. After all we've been through together."

"I serve Smith, as do you," Chiun rejoined. "Smith serves his president. What more is there to be said?"

"Thank you. Now I know where I stand. And what I said earlier still goes. I quit."

"Remo, let me explain," Smith said quickly. "First, what you went through was a contingency operation. Designed simply to get you out of circulation in the event of my being incapacitated. Upon my recovery, you would have been salvaged."

"I love your choice of words," Remo growled, folding his arms.

"It was Ransome's doing that brought you to the brink," Smith went on. "And he has been paid back in his own coin. You did that yourself. That is the end of that. But I have a higher responsibility to America. As you know, in the early days of our association, I had an arrangement with Chiun. Were CURE compromised, and I forced to swallow the poison pill I carry at all times"—Smith extracted a coffin-shaped pill from a pocket of his bathrobe—"it would be his responsibility to end your life quickly and painlessly and then quietly return to Korea. CURE would disappear as if it had never been. No one would ever know that democracy had survived the twentieth century because of our important work."

"Do me a big favor," Remo shot back. "Skip the lecture. My memory's fine now. Too fine."

"If you wish, we can . . . ah . . . edit out all recollections of your recent death-row experiences. There is no need for you to suffer from them."

"No, I'm keeping them. They'll remind me what a prince of a fellow you are, Smith."

Smith cleared his throat. "I devised this contingency plan after the crisis of a few years ago when the Soviets learned of our existence and blackmailed the last president into turning Chiun over to them."

"I remember it well," Remo said acidly.

"As do I," Smith said without rancor. "It was the first time I had been called upon to order you terminated. An order which Master Chiun refused point-blank."

"I did not feel like killing Remo that day," Chiun said officiously. "Not in front of my villagers. They foolishly believe that Remo will support them after I am dust. They would not understand."

"On that day, I took my poison pill. I would have died had it not been for you," Smith said tonelessly.

"I like your concept of reciprocity," Remo remarked dryly.

"You brought me back from the brink of death, but the problem remained. We solved it, you and I. Not as friends, but as uneasy allies. Do not misunderstand our relationship, Remo. I have orders and obligations to my country which come before everything. I will never shirk them as long as I live. But the events of that affair showed me without doubt that the old contingency plan was no longer valid. You have grown beyond your deep-seated patriotism. You are perhaps more Sinanju now than American. And Master Chiun sees you as the heir to Sinanju. You mean more to him than his loyalty to me."

"I could be persuaded to reconsider that attitude," Chiun said hopefully. "For additional gold."

Neither Remo nor Smith looked in Chiun's direction. The Master of Sinanju watched them intently.

"CURE cannot operate without safeguards to prevent our existence from becoming public knowledge," Smith went on. "It is not pleasant, but it is necessary. I hope you will see the events of the last week in that light."

"What I said before still goes," Remo snapped. "I quit. C'mon, Chiun." Remo started for the door. A squeaky voice stopped him in his tracks.

"Write if you get work," Chiun called pleasantly.

Remo turned, his face hurt. "You aren't coming?"

"Alas," Chiun said in a forlorn voice, "I am under contract to Emperor Smith. But do not let that stop you."

Remo hesitated. "I'm really going," he said.

"It is always sad when a child takes off on his own. But perhaps one day you will return." Chiun turned to Smith. "If Remo changes his mind, Emperor, will you forgive him the heartbreak he is causing us both?"

Smith nodded. "Now, if you'll excuse me," he said, "I must return to my office. My examination of Ransome's message-traffic files indicates that our exposure extends to the governor of Florida. I have a very difficult decision to make."

Smith spun his wheelchair about.

"Maybe we should discuss this first," Remo said slowly.

At the door, Smith stopped and turned his head.

"Would you two please take your discussion elsewhere?" he asked. "The technicians need this room."

Smith sent the wheelchair into the swinging door and was gone.

"So," Remo asked Chiun, "where do I stand with you?"

"I will tell Smith whatever he needs to hear, for I accept his gold. But you are the future of my village."

"I'll accept that," Remo said. "For now. You know, he probably has a contingency plan with your name on it too."

Chiun beamed happily. "I am not worried. And rest assured that should any harm befall you due to any action by Smith, he will pay dearly."

"I think Smith understands that."

"You see?" Chiun said, his elfin smile widening.

"And I think he's counting on that," Remo said flatly. "He already took his poison pill once. And he didn't like it. He probably figures you'll be quicker."

Chiun's beaming face quirked. His smile collapsed.

"The fiend!" Chiun flared. "Is there no limit to his craftiness? Come, let us discuss this unpleasantness where the walls do not have ears. And I would like to examine our house for more of Smith's infernal devices. The man is truly a sneak. Invading our very home to work his underhanded schemes."

"All right," Remo said. "I could use a good meal. You wouldn't believe the kind of slop they serve in prison."

"No brown rice?" Chiun asked, aghast. "Only white?"

As they left the room, they passed an attendant wheeling a bundled woman in a wheelchair. Her face was shaded under a wide sunhat.

"Hey!" Remo called as he watched the woman being wheeled into the memory-altering room. "I think that was Naomi. Smith's going to—"

Remo started back. Chiun stopped him.

"It is better than eliminating her," he cautioned.

Remo hesitated. "Guess you're right," he agreed reluctantly. "Besides, she was a twit. Hell of a business we're in, isn't it?"

Chiun shrugged. "It puts duck on the table."

In Starke, Florida, Harold Haines sat in his easy chair, a loaded .38 revolver in his lap. The TV was off. He had not watched it in days. He had not slept in days. His eyes were fixed on the triple-locked door as if on his own tombstone.

"He's coming back," Haines muttered. "I know he is. It's just a matter of time."

He was all alone now. The scuttlebutt was that Warden McSorley had been transferred to Utah. Haines did not believe that. He knew he would be next to disappear. He looked at the weapon in his lap. He picked it up. He wondered if a .38 had enough stopping power to kill a dead man. Did anything have enough stopping power to kill Remo Williams? He shuddered. The answer, of course, was no.

Slowly he placed the oily barrel of the .38 into his mouth. He bit down hard and with his thumb pushed on the trigger.

The report was loud in the tiny motor home. The window in back of Harold Haines's head shattered.

Haines looked down the smoking barrel of the weapon he had yanked from his mouth at the last possible moment. It was like staring down a tunnel without another end.

"I . . . I can't do it!" he sobbed.

Then Harold Haines remembered something he could do. He laid aside the weapon and got his toolbox out from under the sink.

He spent the last evening of his life wiring his favorite easy chair to the portable gasoline generator that sat out in the sultry, mosquito-infested Florida

night. For once, he let the mosquitoes bite him. For
it no longer mattered.

A week later, Remo burst into the front room of
his Rye, New York, home waving a newspaper.

"Hey, Chiun, check this out!" he called.

The Master of Sinanju emerged from the kitchen.
His hazel eyes lit up. Remo's face was free of care.
He was recovering. In time, even the foul tobacco
smoke would be gone from his breath.

"What it is, Remo?" he asked, advancing happily.

"Naomi made the front page," Remo said. He held
up the *National Enquirer*. The headline read: SPACE
ALIENS STEAL RENOWNED ANTHROPOLOGIST'S MEMORY!

Remo turned to an inside page and began reading.

" 'Noted anthropologist Naomi Vanderkloot was discovered wandering dazed through the science building of the University of Massachusetts last Thursday.
When questioned by local authorities, she claimed
not to remember anything that had happened during
the last five years. An *Enquirer* panel of psychics
speculate that space aliens abducted her and sucked
out her memory cells. It is believed that these beings
come from a distant galaxy where the turbulent at-
mosphere prevents ordinary television reception, and
are forced to steal earthling memory cells, which
they play back on VCR-like machines. Similar memory wipes have been reported in Sweden, Rio de
Janeiro and—' "

"Enough," Chiun said. "I do not need to hear any
more of this nonsense. If it amuses you, that is
enough for me."

"Wait," Remo said brightly. "I was just getting to
the best part. Listen: 'Questioned about her plans,
Professor Vanderkloot said that she's organizing a
field trip to the remote Philippine jungles, where
she intends to befriend the semilegendary Moomba
tribe in hopes of solving the riddle of their secret

magic rites.' Isn't that perfect?" Remo asked, laughing uncontrollably.

The Master of Sinanju examined his pupil closely and decided Remo was not necessarily demented.

"White humor," Chiun said, returning to the kitchen. "I will never understand it."